GRIERSON'S RAID

Colonel Benjamin Henry Grierson, commander of the First Brigade, First Cavalry Division, of the Sixteenth Army, U.S. Army. LIBRARY OF CONGRESS

GRIERSON'S RAID

A DARING CAVALRY STRIKE THROUGH
THE HEART OF THE CONFEDERACY

TOM LALICKI

Original maps by David Cain

FARRAR STRAUS GIROUX / NEW YORK

www.fsgkidsbooks.com

Library of Congress Cataloging-in-Publication Data
Lalicki, Tom.
    Grierson's raid : a daring cavalry strike through the heart of the
Confederacy / Tom Lalicki.— 1st ed.
        p. cm.
    Summary: Describes Colonel Benjamin H. Grierson's sixteen-day
raid through central Mississippi in the spring of 1863, which distracted
Confederate attention while Union troops moved on Vicksburg.
    Includes bibliographical references and index.
    ISBN 0-374-32787-4
    1. Grierson's Cavalry Raid, 1863—Juvenile literature.   [1. Grierson's
Cavalry Raid, 1863.   2. Mississippi—History—Civil War, 1861–1865—
Campaigns.   3. United States—History—Civil War, 1861–1865—
Campaigns.]   I. Title.

E475.23.L35 2004
973.7'33—dc22

                                                    2003049253

Contents

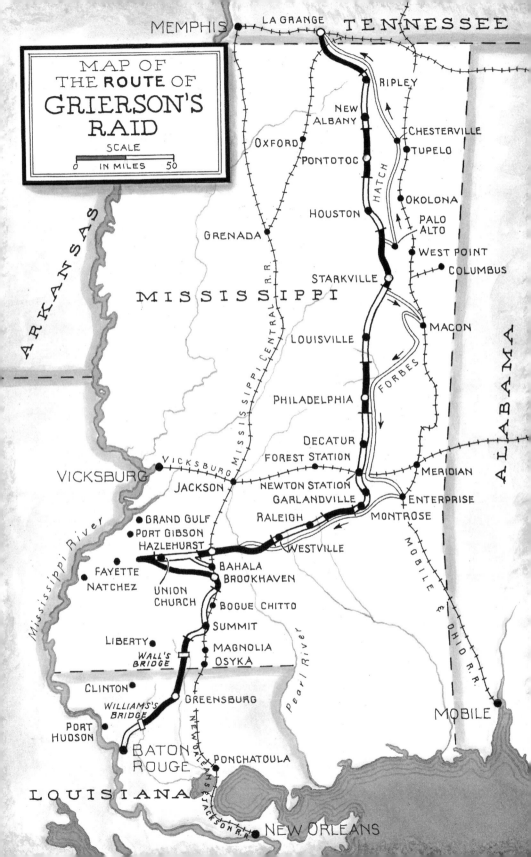

MAP OF
THE ROUTE OF
GRIERSON'S
RAID

SCALE

0   IN MILES   50

MEMPHIS   LA GRANGE   TENNESSEE

RIPLEY

NEW ALBANY

CHESTERVILLE

OXFORD

TUPELO

PONTOTOC

HATCH

HOUSTON

OKOLONA

PALO ALTO

GRENADA

WEST POINT

COLUMBUS

MISSISSIPPI

STARKVILLE

LOUISVILLE

MACON

MISSISSIPPI CENTRAL R.R.

FORBES

PHILADELPHIA

ALABAMA

DECATUR

FOREST STATION

VICKSBURG

MERIDIAN

JACKSON

NEWTON STATION

GARLANDVILLE

ENTERPRISE

VICKSBURG

RALEIGH

MONTROSE

GRAND GULF

WESTVILLE

PORT GIBSON

HAZLEHURST

MOBILE & OHIO R.R.

FAYETTE

BAHALA

NATCHEZ

BROOKHAVEN

UNION CHURCH

BOGUE CHITTO

Mississippi River

SUMMIT

LIBERTY

MAGNOLIA

OSYKA

WALL'S BRIDGE

CLINTON

GREENSBURG

Pearl River

WILLIAMS'S BRIDGE

PORT HUDSON

BATON ROUGE

PONCHATOULA

NEW ORLEANS & JACKSON R.R.

LOUISIANA

MOBILE

NEW ORLEANS

Self-preservation is the first law of nature. The man who does not dread to die or to be mutilated is a lunatic. The man who, dreading these things, still faces them for the sake of duty and honor is a hero.
—John W. De Forest, Civil War veteran

"RETURN IMMEDIATELY!"

"Return immediately!" was the telegram's entire message. It was the only message Colonel Benjamin H. Grierson needed. Something big was afoot in Mississippi, a military operation that had been planned secretly for months, and Grierson had a vital part to play in it.

It was April 13, 1863; the Civil War was fully two years old. In April 1861, Grierson had volunteered to fight what most Northerners thought would be a short and glorious war to preserve the Union. But the Confederates were a determined enemy. Far from surrendering, the South seemed to be winning.

The year 1862 had been a terrible one for the Union. A Federal assault on Richmond, Virginia, the Confederate capital, failed miserably. Northern troops were decisively beaten at Second Bull Run. Then General Robert E. Lee's army escaped to Virginia after the catastrophic standoff at Antietam, where more than twenty-three thousand Americans were killed or wounded on a single day. Months later, another massive battle at Fredericksburg, Virginia, left nearly eighteen thousand men dead or dying with no advantage gained by either side.

In the western war theater, General Ulysses S. Grant's victories in Tennessee were neutralized by two stunning defeats in Mississippi—Chickasaw Bayou and Holly Springs. The following year began with a costly Union victory at Stones River in middle Tennessee. After a three-day battle that started on December 31, 1862, the Confederate army retreated with 33 percent of its soldiers dead, wounded, or missing. The Federal side lost 31 percent of its army. But it was a moment when victory, however bloody, however fleeting, was a cause for joy. "God bless you and all with you," President Abraham Lincoln wrote the commanding general. "You gave us a hard victory which, had there been a defeat instead, the nation could scarcely have lived over."

Public opinion in the North had turned against the war. *Harper's Weekly*, the national news magazine, accused Northern leadership of "imbecility, treachery, failure." Other newspapers were calling for an armistice, a truce to stop the war indefinitely. A leading Federal general said, "Exhaustion steals over the country. Confidence and hope are dying."

Even as winter weather brought a halt to the fighting, General Grant relentlessly pursued President Lincoln's plan of splitting the Confederacy in two by reclaiming the Mississippi River. Union forces had already won back the river from Illinois down to Vicksburg, Mississippi, and from New Orleans north nearly to Vicksburg. Lincoln had told his generals that "Vicksburg is the key . . . The war can never be brought to a close until that key is in our pocket." But it would not fall easily; Jefferson Davis, president of the Confederacy, had told his generals to defend Vicksburg "at all costs."

A prosperous port before the war, Vicksburg by 1863 had become an armed fortress. The city was built on an unassail-

Major General Ulysses S. Grant, commander of the Department of the Tennessee. His mission was the capture of Vicksburg, Mississippi. A diversionary raid by Grierson was an essential part of his plans. JAMES WADSWORTH FAMILY PAPERS, LIBRARY OF CONGRESS MANUSCRIPT DIVISION

able two-hundred-foot cliff above the Mississippi's eastern shore—a commanding spot for artillery. Large guns that could sink practically any ship prevented navigation up or down the river. Trenches and fortifications manned by thirty thousand troops ringed the city. Strong forces to the east at Jackson and to the south at Grand Gulf made any approach difficult.

Vicksburg was better defended than any other Southern city because it was a vital transportation hub. The Vicksburg &

Southern Railroad ran from the river east to a series of north–south railroads. Beef, pork, and corn from Arkansas and Texas were distributed throughout the eastern Confederate states from Vicksburg; cotton from Mississippi and sugar from Louisiana also passed through the city. Vicksburg fed and clothed the Confederacy; it *was* the key to Union victory.

During the winter of 1862, General Grant tried, and failed at, a number of approaches. An invasion from the north was repulsed. Attempts to dig canals in the swamps of Arkansas that would float his troops safely past Vicksburg's big guns foundered. After months of failure, the Northern army in Mississippi was fatigued and frustrated. A captain under Grant wrote: "I never in my life saw such a change in an Army . . . Men, Officers, who 60 days ago were in favor of fighting till the last man . . . are now in favor of Compromise." Another wrote home saying he was "very much discouraged . . . I have lost all my enthusiasm, a large portion of my patriotism and all my confidence."

Never losing hope, Grant patiently plotted a daring new strategy in February 1863. A squadron of armored gunboats and transport ships carrying food, ammunition, and other supplies would cruise past Vicksburg's artillery under cover of darkness. More than twenty-three thousand Federal soldiers would march through the wetlands on the western bank of the river and meet the ships far south of Vicksburg. Protected by a barrage of fire from the Union gunboats, the infantrymen would be ferried across the river and land on the Vicksburg side. General William Tecumseh Sherman would remain upriver with seventeen thousand soldiers slated to march down the eastern bank and assault the northern end of Vicksburg.

Unaided, the plan would never work. Anticipating the general location of Grant's forces, Confederate cavalry would patrol the riverbank and send out alarms long before the crossing happened. Confederate infantry and artillery would be moved in place to slaughter the vulnerable soldiers before they touched land.

The only hope for success was diverting Confederate attention away from the river, creating a distraction that alarmed

The Vicksburg piers were a beehive of commercial activity in normal times. People and goods flowed in and out in all directions. LIBRARY OF CONGRESS

and confused all the Confederate commanders in Mississippi. A fast-moving, skillfully led cavalry raid through the heart of central Mississippi, a raid that ripped down telegraph lines, destroyed railroad tracks, burned bridges, and frightened citizens, could do the trick. And Grant knew that Ben Grierson was the soldier to lead that raid. "It seems to me that Grierson," Grant wrote on February 13, "with about 500 picked men, might

Batteries of artillery ringed the city of Vicksburg to keep Union attackers out. More than one hundred cannon were mounted on the city walls. These Parrott guns weighed nearly ten thousand pounds and could fire a shell more than a mile. LIBRARY OF CONGRESS

succeed . . . The undertaking would be a hazardous one, but it would pay well if carried out. I do not direct that this shall be done, but leave it for a volunteer enterprise."

Grierson agreed enthusiastically, and the plan was under way. Camped fifty miles east of Memphis, Tennessee, in La Grange, Colonel Grierson maintained strong confidence and hope in the Union cause during what he called "a very gloomy winter." Mud and rain kept his cavalry troopers inactive, cold, and wet; measles kept many in the hospital. Two years of separation from his wife and children depressed but didn't defeat him. That winter he wrote his wife, Alice, a love poem more than one hundred lines long, closing with these thoughts:

To see you again soon I have faith that I will,
And to find you, as ever, in love with me still . . .
May your pathway be strewn with bright blooming flowers,
May God protect, and cheer you, in your lonely hours;
Let our hearts grow with warmth, and never be colder,
As the time passes on and in years we grow older.

When Grierson did see Alice again, it was only days before his perilous ride was scheduled to begin—and he couldn't even fill her in. Secrecy was so important that "not one word was breathed aloud" about the details. Fearful of spies, Grierson's commander, General Stephen A. Hurlbut, officially recorded Grierson's absence from camp as a mission to deliver regimental dispatches. Grierson's cue was merely two words: "Return immediately!"

He did. Taking a train to St. Louis, then a river steamer to Memphis and another train to La Grange, Grierson had three days to contemplate the mission. But he may have thought

more about the strong possibility that it was his last sight of
family and friends. "That visit home was one of the most en-
joyable experiences of my life" was how Grierson remembered
it nearly thirty years later in his autobiography. "It was an oasis
of love in the midst of a desert of doubt, darkness and uncertainty. A person only who has determined upon some perilous
adventure . . . can realise the extreme rapture that filled my
heart at being once more surrounded by the kind loving hearts
of home."

Waiting for a connecting train in Memphis, Grierson was
given his final orders by General Hurlbut verbally. They were
vague, because Hurlbut thought the mission too hazardous to

take the responsibility for giving definite orders for its execution. Grierson would command a cavalry brigade—three regiments of horsemen and a battery of artillery. The brigade would leave La Grange, Tennessee, with roughly seventeen hundred men and their horses. Its objective was to destroy the Vicksburg & Jackson Railroad at Newton Station, Mississippi. Grierson was ordered to damage any other military targets he found along the way. To get back to base, he was ordered to use his own discretion.

By the spring of 1863, the hills inside Vicksburg's fortifications had become crisscrossed with trenches. More than thirty thousand Confederate troops could defend the city from a land attack. LIBRARY OF CONGRESS

Accepting the grave responsibility, Grierson penned this optimistic letter to Alice from Memphis: "My command is ordered to leave La Grange to-morrow . . . We will be gone probably *three weeks*, and perhaps longer . . . If I have any opportunity to write to you I will do so; but you must not be alarmed, should you not hear from me inside of a month. I have a faith and hope that I will return all right . . . If the expedition is successful, it will be of great benefit to the service . . . Write to me occasionally: even if I do not get the letters when they arrive at La Grange, it will be a pleasure to have a number to read on my return . . . And now dear Alice, think of our pleasant visit which we luckily have had, and try to be cheerful and happy."

Grierson's poetry and letter writing may seem out of keeping with his military status, but he wasn't unique in the Civil War. Grierson was just one of 700,000 Northern men with no military experience or ambition who enlisted in 1861. But he had a very unexpected past for a cavalry officer.

Grierson disliked horses. He never trusted them. At the age of eight, he had been kicked in the head by a horse. Lucky not to die, he spent weeks in a coma. After waking up, he couldn't see. Finally, when his sight returned months after the accident, he discovered a scar that ran down his face from below an eye to his chin—a permanent reminder that horses were dangerous.

After enlisting and being commissioned a lieutenant, he was horrified to be assigned to the cavalry—the horse army. Grierson asked for reassignment, but a general decided that he was "active and wiry" enough to be a good cavalryman. So the tall, thin, loose-boned son of Irish immigrants who always wore a full beard to cover his facial scar taught himself about the cavalry from training manuals he bought in bookstores. In October 1861, Governor Richard Yates made him a major in the Sixth Illinois Cavalry Regiment. Fellow officers were impressed by Grierson's leadership and bravery. In April 1862, thirty-seven regimental officers petitioned the governor, recommending Grierson's further promotion. The governor appointed him colonel that month. In December 1862, General Grant recognized Grierson's extraordinary talents and gave him command of a brigade, three regiments of cavalry.

Colonel Grierson had the total confidence of his superiors. One said that he "was an ideal cavalry officer—brave and dashing, cunning and resourceful." He would need to be all that and more on the ride through Mississippi. Once his troopers passed into Mississippi, the brigade would be completely on its own. The fastest forms of communication in this era before telephones were the telegraph and horse-riding couriers. Both would be unavailable to Grierson deep behind enemy lines; both could help the Confederates pinpoint his location, though. If the brigade rode three hundred miles to the Vicksburg Railroad without being discovered, it would be hundreds of miles from safety in any direction and surrounded by up to fifty thousand potential attackers.

It was after midnight on the morning of April 17, 1863, when Grierson finally reached camp in La Grange. Ablaze with torchlight, the camp seethed with activity. Troopers were busy with final packing, feeding and watering of horses, and counting off and lining up into squadrons for inspection. Grierson met with his senior officers and briefed them on the mission. Only Lieutenant Samuel Woodward, his adjutant, or communications officer, was given all the details at that time. Never commanding troops in battle, the adjutant was the officer least likely to be killed or captured. If Grierson fell, Wood-ward would relay the plans to his successor.

That night, nobody in La Grange knew that the first step of Grant's two-pronged offensive against Vicksburg had already succeeded. Six Federal gunboats had steamed past Vicksburg's deadly artillery fire around midnight. Taking hundreds of direct hits, all six ships survived to dock far south of the city on the river's western bank. Grant's infantry was already sloughing through swamp, marching down the pathless west bank to meet the boats. By Grant's calculations, his army would be ready in a week or so to ferry across the river, conquer the Confederate base at Grand Gulf, and begin the final march to Vicksburg—if Grierson's raid worked.

As night turned to day, Grierson attended to last-minute details. He had been too busy that night to pencil a hasty note home or to catch even a few moments of sleep.

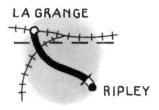

LA GRANGE

RIPLEY

DAY ONE: FRIDAY, APRIL 17

⭐ "Just as the sun rose full and fine over a charming expanse of small pine-clad hills, the first brigade, stretching itself out from the little village, slid like a huge serpent into the cover of the Mississippi woods." That's how Sergeant Stephen Forbes remembered the raiders' dawn departure from La Grange. At nineteen years old, Forbes was an old-timer, a hardened veteran. After seeing combat several times, he had been captured by the Confederates in Mississippi. During his four months in a prisoner-of-war camp, Forbes contracted malaria and scurvy and suffered from malnutrition. Released to Federal forces in critical condition, he was conveyed to a hospital in Rhode Island and recuperated there for three months. Fiercely committed to the cause of union, Forbes rejoined the Seventh and was promoted to sergeant in Company B, serving under his brother, Captain Henry Forbes.

Stephen Forbes had no doubts about the righteousness of the war. He had no questions about his role in it. In one letter home, he used the word "duty" five times in one sentence. But like most of his comrades, Forbes had mixed feelings about the slow, painful pacification of the Southern states. In a letter

written to his sister two nights before the raid, he said: "There is just haze enough to tone down the moonlight to the most beautiful dreaminess, to hide every distortion and beautify every grace of landscape . . . Perhaps it seems a little strange that we should think anything about pleasant weather, we, who have come down here to kill our fellows and carry distress to families, to dislocate the country and destroy life by wholesale."

Forbes's "huge serpent"—officially the First Brigade, First Cavalry Division, Sixteenth Army Corps of Major General Ulysses S. Grant's Department of the Tennessee—rode in columns of twos into deep evergreen-covered forest. The brigade comprised three volunteer cavalry regiments—the Sixth Illinois, the Seventh Illinois, and the Second Iowa—and a detachment of six mounted two-pounder cannon known as Woodruff guns from the First Illinois Artillery. To disguise the size of its force and reduce the length of its march, the brigade separated into two columns. The Sixth Illinois journeyed by itself on the main road; the Seventh Illinois and Second Iowa split off several miles to the east and turned southward on a parallel trail. Both columns marched at the unhurried, standard cavalry pace of three miles per hour, stopping five to ten minutes each hour to water and rest the horses.

"Some were singing, others laughing, while many were speculating as to our destination," Sergeant Richard Surby of the Seventh wrote in his journal, and most "were spoiling for a fight." Given the limited rations and ammunition they carried, most probably agreed with Surby's guess that they were "go-

Stephen Alfred Forbes was seventeen years old when he volunteered to serve in the Seventh Illinois Cavalry. UNIVERSITY ARCHIVES, UNIVERSITY OF ILLINOIS AT URBANA-CHAMPAIGN

ing on a big scout to Columbus, Mississippi, and play smash
with the railroads."

From his own experiences, Sergeant Stephen Forbes had
good reason to fear another dangerous ride into Mississippi,
but clearly he didn't. Forty-four years after the raid, he remembered his comrades proudly as "seasoned soldiers, most of
them, well mounted and well armed, fresh from a winter's rest
in camp (if cavalry can ever be said to rest), gay with youth
and the hope of fresh adventure, with no baggage to encum-
ber them save what was strapped to their saddles, carrying
each forty rounds of ammunition, five days' rations and a good
supply of salt, they were an exceptionally fit party for a hard
and rapid cavalry raid."

If the raiders seemed high-spirited and optimistic during the
Union's season of despair and doubt, Grierson's leadership
was the primary cause. When the Civil War began, practically
none of the officers in either the Federal or the Confederate
armies had any previous military experience. They learned the
craft of soldiering in the process of teaching it to enlisted men.
Some officers were naturally better soldiers and leaders than
others. Many never realized that morale was always low
among undisciplined soldiers. Other officers could not develop
the strength to command "citizen soldiers." As one historian
wrote, "American white males were the most individualistic,
democratic people on the face of the earth in 1861. They did
not take kindly to authority, discipline, obedience." Grierson
understood that: "It required both moral and physical courage
to bring about the marked improvement in the rough western
men of my regiment, who were inclined to fight [rather] than
obey orders."

From the day Ben Grierson arrived at the Sixth's Shawneetown, Illinois, headquarters, the men took to his leadership. "I found everything connected with the command in great confusion with but little signs of discipline or system. The regiment had never been drilled," he remembered. "I organized a school for the officers and gave theoretical and practical instruction daily . . . The [battalion] drills were kept up every day when the weather would permit and inspection and dress parades held on Sundays." Grierson showed concern for his troopers' personal comfort and welfare as well. He requisitioned new tents, had proper latrines built, bought quality horses, gave troopers leave to visit home, and required officers to live in camp with the men. Other troopers in the Sixth envied those in Grierson's hard-worked, tightly disciplined battalion. It was less than two months later that the regiment's officers wrote their letter to the governor of Illinois recommending Grierson's promotion to colonel.

Concern for the welfare of common soldiers and the ability to lead were two of the qualities necessary to inspire confidence in Civil War armies; the third was personal courage. Soldiers were more willing to risk their lives if their commanders shared the risk equally. Grierson did; he seemed unfazed by personal danger in battle. When four hundred Confederate cavalrymen swooped down on his dismounted regiment in 1862, Grierson immediately rallied his resting troopers to horse. Wearing a long white coat that made him a very obvious target, he formed his troopers into a battle line and counterattacked. The Sixth eventually routed the attackers, but not before Grierson took two shots through his coat, one through his pant leg, and another that ripped several fingers.

An observer in Grierson's camp captured the spirit: "There appears to be a mutual satisfaction between Ben and his men as to his and their conduct. They say they have a brave colonel and he says that he has the best fighting regiment of cavalry in the service."

Being the "best fighting regiment of cavalry" was faint praise in most circles. A favorite joke in the Union army ran, "If you want to have a good time, join the cavalry. Nobody ever saw a dead cavalryman." In 1863, an infantryman in Tennessee summed up the Union cavalry's efforts this way: "I really have as yet to see or hear of their doing anything of much credit to them." When compared with the dashing exploits of Confederate cavalry units led by well-known officers like John Hunt Morgan, Nathan Bedford Forrest, and Jeb Stuart, the Union cavalry had done little. But it had started the race far behind.

At the war's outset, U.S. Commanding General Winfield Scott thought that the cavalry was outmoded and unnecessary. Reasoning that no cavalry could charge against modern cannon fire, he discouraged the formation of cavalry regiments. When General George McClellan took command of the army in July 1861, more units were established, but they were poorly supplied. Equipment was so scarce that many cavalry units "played" at being soldiers. A letter home from Captain Henry Forbes illustrates the point: "We have not drilled on horse yet, for the reason we have no saddles. We have daily foot drills, however, and shall soon be furnished in full." In those early days, Ben Grierson spent much of his time traveling from warehouse to warehouse in search of rifles, saddles, and other vital equipment.

Union cavalry was initially limited to messenger and escort

This Federal army camp in southern Tennessee probably looked much like the camp in La Grange. Because their tents were used as winter quarters, the soldiers built log walls to make them less drafty. LIBRARY OF CONGRESS

duties. By 1863, Federal cavalry had taken on three primary responsibilities: patrolling in front of and on the flanks of a marching army to prevent surprise attacks; reconnaissance or stealth patrolling to discover the position or strength of the enemy; and raiding or "making mischief" behind enemy lines. Ammunition and supplies moved by railroad, and most communication was done by telegraph; damaging railroads and telegraphs could make an army helpless.

But Northern cavalry was also inferior, at first, to Southern for cultural reasons—Southerners loved horses. Southern boys learned to ride very young and continued to ride all their lives because public roads were poor and railroads were few. Pro-

fessional horse racing and hunting on horseback were popular
Southern sports. Cavalry tactics were taught at the South's numerous military academies. Union General William Tecumseh
Sherman taught at a Louisiana academy before the war and
said of his pupils: "They are splendid riders, first-rate shots, and
utterly reckless . . . They are the best cavalry in the world."

Boys in New England and the Midwest grew up riding in
buggies or spent their days walking behind plow horses. Fast,
maneuverable horses were rare in the North because horse
racing was almost nonexistent. Horsemanship was not a common trait in Iowa or Illinois. But after two years of training under fire, the Federals were catching up. The men of the First
Brigade, riding to an unknown destination on an undefined
mission that sunny spring day, were confident of their abilities.

The morning and afternoon passed without incident. Occasionally the raiders sped up to a trot to relieve muscle fatigue
in the horses. They passed civilians who took little notice. Mississippi residents just south of the Tennessee border were
accustomed to seeing Union soldiers on the move. Colonel
Edward Prince, commander of the Seventh, came upon a Mississippi farm boy crying along the side of the road. Asking the
reason, Prince learned that when the Seventh's advance patrol
had encountered the youth minutes earlier, "he wore a very
good looking hat which one of the boys took a fancy to and
relieved him of, leaving the poor fellow looking rather sad,"
one raider observed. The poor fellow's mood improved when
Colonel Prince gave him a U.S. two-dollar bill.

The first day's unhurried, worry-free ride ended with a fore-
taste of the danger ahead. As the columns re-formed to camp
on a plantation north of Ripley, Mississippi, six Confederates
were spotted observing the raiders from a distance. Taking

chase, Grierson's troopers captured three of them. The three who got away undoubtedly sent out an alarm that night: "The Yankees are coming!"

While Grierson questioned the prisoners, his commissary sergeants methodically "raided" the plantation's smokehouse and storage barn. As coffee boiled over dozens of open fires, the men enjoyed rations of ham and smoked turkey with their meal of hardtack biscuits; the horses had corn and hay with their water. Using saddles for pillows and raincoats for blankets, the Federal cavalry troopers rested peacefully that warm spring night.

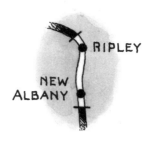

RIPLEY

NEW ALBANY

DAY TWO: SATURDAY, APRIL 18

⭐ As dawn broke, sentries rode back into camp. They had only minutes to grab cups of hot coffee and a snack of cold meat before falling into line for the day's march. Led by Colonel Prince's Seventh Illinois, the raiders took the road to Ripley, Mississippi, in columns of two. The Sixth Illinois, commanded by Colonel Reuben Loomis since Grierson's promotion, fell in behind. Captain Jason Smith's Battery K, First Illinois Artillery, slipped into the line ahead of Colonel Edward Hatch's Second Iowa Cavalry.

Altogether, it was an incredibly long, thin, vulnerable line of mounted men traveling down the narrow, dusty dirt road. Even riding two abreast, nearly seventeen hundred mounted men cannot be kept secret very long. The column should have been nearly twice as long. The First Brigade was only at half strength, but Grierson was fortunate to have more than five hundred men in each of his three regiments. Many Federal regiments took the field in 1863 with two hundred men or even fewer.

Federal regiments started out the war fully staffed, but death, severe wounds, sickness, and desertion reduced their numbers.

All new soldiers were recruited, until late 1863, at the state level. Instead of those soldiers being fed into existing regiments, new units were formed. While putting a manpower strain on units like the Sixth Illinois, the system helped them too. Troopers lived, worked, and fought together for months and years at a time. They developed mutual respect and dependence on each other. Their closeness was enhanced further because of prewar personal ties. It was common for all the members of a company to hail from the same town or county. Many, like the two Forbes brothers of Company B, were related.

Working and fighting together well would help the raiders survive battle, but accomplishing their mission was another matter. They had nearly three hundred miles of enemy territory to cross before reaching their goal. From there, it was hundreds of miles in any direction to safety. General Grant had not sent Grierson's brigade on a suicide mission, though. He relied on two different military elements to make the raid successful: a coordinated series of diversionary attacks and Grierson's superior generalship.

The first element was already in play. Four more Federal cavalry and mixed cavalry and infantry forces were moving from Tennessee toward Confederate positions in Mississippi. These were "demonstrations," shows of force intended to distract the enemy's attention away from the real point of attack: Grierson's movement southward. Three of the Union demonstrations accomplished their purpose, occupying Confederate forces for a few days until the Union armies turned and briskly retreated.

The fourth Federal demonstration proved a disaster. A rebel force commanded by Confederate General Nathan Bedford Forrest quickly intersected a Union cavalry regiment under

Colonel Abel Streight. Outmanned by a superior force, Streight's troopers skirmished for two weeks until the entire regiment surrendered in Georgia.

While these demonstrations provided the raiders with valuable cover for their movements, they would face the same fate unless Grierson's judgment and decision making were perfect. How extraordinary and dire a time it was when the lives of thousands were entrusted to the military talents of a bandleader.

After the childhood riding accident that nearly killed him, young Ben Grierson developed a passion for music. "Long before I played on any instrument I used to amuse myself and others by singing and whistling and . . . drumming," he remembered in his 1892 autobiography. After mastering a child-sized flute, he learned to play clarinet, bugle, and the bass drum. By the age of twelve, he had been elected leader of his hometown band, but still he couldn't get enough music. "I would plead for permission of the band members to use their instruments and seemingly by intuition could play with ease on all." Eventually he mastered the guitar, violin, and piano.

A good student who liked reading William Shakespeare's plays and poets like Lord Byron and John Keats, Grierson applied for and won an appointment to West Point, the United States Military Academy. His mother pleaded with him to stick with music, so he did. After graduating from the local school, Grierson stayed in Jacksonville and taught music. But music did not pay well. There was not much demand for musical instruction in the agricultural frontier country of 1850s Illinois; farmers did not have much money to pay for it either.

In 1854, when he was twenty-eight, Grierson had a chance meeting with his childhood sweetheart, Alice Kirk. That encounter rekindled their love, and they were married shortly after. To provide for his wife and growing family, Grierson abandoned music and went into general merchandise. With a partner, he opened a store in the river town of Meredosia, Illinois, far from his home in Jacksonville.

Grierson and his partner were not wise or lucky businessmen. They sold too much on credit, and when a business slowdown struck the country, they could not raise enough cash from customers to pay their debts. The store was bankrupt, and Grierson had fallen deeply into debt by 1860. He re-

This 1854 photograph of the Grierson family is probably a wedding portrait. Seated from the left are brothers John C. Grierson and Benjamin H. Grierson. Their wives, Elizabeth and Alice, are standing. FORT DAVIS NATIONAL HISTORIC SITE, NATIONAL PARK SERVICE

turned to Jacksonville "without a dollar" and with no viable way to support his growing family.

While in Meredosia, Grierson had become an ardent follower of the recently formed Republican Party and its Illinois standard-bearer, Abraham Lincoln. The future president stayed at Grierson's house after debating in Meredosia, and Grierson later wrote the campaign song for Lincoln's 1860 presidential race. When Lincoln won, Grierson said, "No person in the land rejoiced . . . more than myself."

In April 1861, secessionists bombarded Fort Sumter into surrender, and Grierson's path was clear: "I determined to go into the army in any event, either as an aide to a general officer; an officer of the line; chief musician of a regiment . . . or as a private soldier in the ranks." Serving eight months as an unpaid volunteer, Grierson fed himself and his family on a bank loan while he tirelessly studied army regulations, law, strategy, and the geography and topography of the South. He must have realized that leading a cavalry regiment required the same skills as leading a band: knowing the subject, presenting it clearly, and expecting orders to be followed.

Perhaps the most important reason for choosing Grierson to lead the raid was General Sherman's profound confidence in the colonel's leadership abilities. "Colonel Grierson," the general bragged, "always goes with his men wherever sent; is invariably successful in accomplishing orders and bringing in his command safely." The raid would be a failure if half the brigade members were casualties—wounded or killed—and the other half languished in prison camp. Generals Grant and Sherman wanted Grierson to rip up the railroad and distract the Confederates, but they wanted him to bring the brigade home safely, too.

After an hour's march, the Seventh trooped into Ripley without incident. Neither Confederate soldiers nor armed civilians met them—just a few cautious townspeople curiously watching the streets fill with blue-uniformed soldiers. Grierson's orders to the regimental commanders made it clear that the straightforward part of their journey was over; the game of deception was beginning.

The only practical route south put the raiders on a course parallel to two strongly defended north–south railroads: the combined Mississippi Central/New Orleans & Jackson to the west and the Mobile & Ohio to the east. Confederate General James Chalmers, with a force of one thousand cavalrymen, was responsible for patrolling the western side of the state and the Mississippi Central rail line. Confederate General Daniel Ruggles, with a command of more than two thousand, protected the eastern side of the state and the Mobile & Ohio. Pickets, small detached bodies of troops, patrolled the entire length of those railroads. The raiders' line of march brought them within easy reach of this Confederate reconnaissance. Once discovered, the brigade would be exposed to flank attacks and ambushes from both front and rear. Delaying tactics like that would give the Confederates time to position overwhelming force ahead of Grierson, eradicating any chance for success. And overwhelming force was available. Chalmers and Ruggles reported to the overall commander for Mississippi, General John C. Pemberton, who had more than forty thousand troops available in the Jackson-Vicksburg area. There were twenty thousand infantrymen and twelve hundred cavalrymen at Port Hudson, Louisiana, and another twelve thousand soldiers at Grand Gulf; Colonel William Wirt Adams held Port Gibson with a regiment of cavalry. Together, they were the forces that General Grant hoped Grierson would attract to his raid. Grierson's challenge was to draw their attention without getting caught. He needed to mislead, confuse, and distract the Confederates, not fight them.

Leaving Ripley, Colonel Hatch's Second Iowa marched east toward a station on the Mobile & Ohio Railroad. The Illinois regiments under Loomis and Prince took the road south toward New Albany. Grierson knew that if a civilian messenger from Ripley reached Confederate troopers with word about the raiders, reinforcements would be sent to protect the railroad. Informants couldn't know that Hatch's orders were to proceed east only four miles, turn south on a path parallel to Grierson's, and rejoin the brigade later.

Suddenly, four miles south of Ripley, eight Confederate cavalry riders fired on an advance scouting party of the Seventh. Instinctively, the Federals charged their attackers, then quickly stopped and doubled back—they might have been riding into an ambush. When Colonel Prince arrived, he decided to make a countermove. The Confederates may have been a detached party or scouts for a larger force; he couldn't know. Prince did know that the brigade needed to cross a Tallahatchie River bridge twelve miles forward at New Albany to stay on schedule. Rebel defenders could already be amassing there. Prince dispatched Major John Graham and a full battalion, at a gallop, with orders to take and hold the bridge.

Heightened emotions—the awareness of danger—pulsed through the Seventh. The Sixth, so far back that its troopers didn't hear the shots fired, continued on at the customary march speed. Hatch's Second Iowa was just turning south after its feint at the railroad when it was fired on.

Scouts from the First Mississippi Regiment, a state home

guard, attacked the Iowa regiment's advance party. Very quickly, the Mississippi soldiers realized they were outmanned and outgunned. The Confederate Conscription Act of 1862 had placed most healthy young Southern men in the regular army; others hid in the woods to avoid the draft. The home guards were exempt from conscription, either too young, too old, or too ill. Riding farm horses and toting shotguns and ancient muskets, they were no match for the Second Iowa. Nonetheless, they skirmished with Hatch's regiment for hours and retarded his march. At nightfall, the Iowans were forced to make camp alone, far short of the day's goal. Hatch ordered double sentries that night, certain that his attackers had sent a rider to warn General Ruggles's headquarters about the Yankee cavalry.

When the troopers commanded by Major Graham galloped up to the Tallahatchie bridge, they found pickets guarding it. A full-blooded cavalry charge by the Federals made the pickets take to horse, but it was too late for four who were easily captured. While Graham held the bridge, Grierson and the Sixth forded a shallow part of the river upstream. By late afternoon, the Illinois regiments had re-formed in New Albany and were awaiting the Iowans. Sergeant Surby of the Seventh observed that New Albany was "a small place composed of a few dry-goods stores, whose stock needed replenishing." Shortages had become common in the South by 1863.

Five miles south of New Albany, the Illinois regiments made camp miles away from the second Iowa. Grierson quizzed the four prisoners brought in from the Tallahatchie bridge. Two were attached to a home-guard unit, but the others were regular soldiers from Lieutenant Colonel Clark Barteau's Second Tennessee Cavalry, a unit under General Ruggles's command.

Colonel Edward Hatch, commander of the Second Iowa. Before the war, Hatch was a lumber merchant. ROGER D. HUNT COLLECTION AT THE U.S. ARMY MILITARY HISTORY INSTITUTE

They obligingly told Grierson that Barteau was less than twenty miles away with five hundred regular cavalrymen and nearly as many state troops—a formidable force that had to be distracted. Barteau was responsible, first, for guarding the Mobile & Ohio Railroad and, second, for routing Federal raiders who might try to inflict damage on Mississippi. Barteau was Grierson's designated foe.

The raiders' natural foe—bad weather—rolled in that evening. Thunder and lightning got the men working to improvise shelter. Fences were torn apart, the rails used as makeshift "mattresses." Dry brush was piled up for the same purpose. The liberties being taken with his property infuriated the plantation's owner, a Mr. Sloan. Grierson remembered events this way: "As usual, we demanded the keys of smokehouses and barns, food for men and horses. Mr. Sloan wanted in a small way to resist where resistance was of course impossible; would not give up his keys until the locks were broken. When he saw his stores issued out, he was completely beside himself; alternately was going to cut my throat, and desirous of having his own throat cut." When Mr. Sloan saw troopers driving a herd of horses and mules from their hiding place in the woods, his agitation rose even higher. "He fairly foamed, and for the fiftieth time demanded that we take him out and cut his throat and be done with it." Ben Grierson, the spirited performer, was unable to resist a little acting at this point. "Mr. Sloan is very desirous of having his throat cut," Grierson told his orderly. "Take him out in the field and *cut his throat, and be done with it.*" The orderly unsheathed a long, sharp knife and grabbed the plantation owner's collar. "Now began a hubbub. Mrs. Sloan, who all along had been more self-possessed than her husband, . . . began to scream in chorus with the servants."

The threatening play continued until Sloan promised to be quiet if his life was spared. Quiet was all that Grierson really wanted anyway.

"Horses had to be pressed [into service] whenever and wherever found, and in many instances double the number were left for those taken," as Sergeant Surby noted in his daily journal. Seeing the horses that Grierson left behind the next day gave Sloan the last laugh. Sloan was satisfied that "he had the best of the trade with the Yankees after all," Grierson observed later in his autobiography.

NEW
ALBANY

PONTOTOC

DAY THREE: SUNDAY, APRIL 19

"The rain fell in torrents all night," according to Grierson. It slackened to a steady downpour by dawn. Any troopers still asleep when the bugle played reveille that morning realized at once that they had a wet, uncomfortable day ahead of them. Every item of clothing a trooper wore, except for boots, was made of moisture-absorbent wool: blue cap, dark-blue dress jacket and blouse, light-blue reinforced trousers, flannel shirt, underwear, and socks. His only rain protection was the poncho—a large piece of partially waterproof cotton with a hole cut in its center. Pulled down over his shoulders, a poncho kept most of a man dry, but let the rain run down his chest and back. And riding was treacherous on sloppy clay roads; horses could lose their footing easily.

During breakfast with his staff, Grierson ordered a series of diversions to begin the day. "I sent a detachment eastward to communicate with Colonel Hatch and make a demonstration toward Chesterville [near Tupelo], where a regiment of cavalry was organizing. I also sent an expedition to New Albany, and another northwest toward King's Bridge, to attack and destroy a portion of a regiment of cavalry organizing there . . . I thus sought to create the impression that the object of our advance was to break up these parties." So three detachments, two companies in each, moved north—away from their eventual objective—at 6 a.m. The remainder of the Sixth and Seventh stayed behind at Mr. Sloan's plantation to enjoy a leisurely breakfast and improvised Sunday morning prayer services.

The first detachment, led by Captain George Trafton, rode slowly back to New Albany. The troopers were surprised to discover that nearly one hundred Mississippi state soldiers had occupied the town overnight. Sighting Trafton's advance party, the Mississippians positioned themselves for a fight. Trafton obliged them by signaling an all-out charge down the main street. Riding at a gallop, the raiders first fired into the enemy, then holstered their carbines, drew sabers, and slashed forward. In very short order, the defenders broke into full retreat. Just as quickly as those Mississippi state soldiers were dispersed, Trafton turned his detachment south again—mission accomplished.

The second detachment had an equal but different kind of success at King's Bridge. It found the enemy camp deserted. Fires still smoldered, and bedding was left unrolled in tents; the enemy had departed in a hurry. Some of the raiders spread out to scour the soggy farmland nearby for stragglers. The rest set to burning down the camp—not an easy task in a downpour. Eventually, they all headed back to the rendezvous point.

The third detachment picked its way very slowly toward its goal—communicating orders to Hatch's Second Iowa. The troopers were unaware that the Iowans had drawn heavy fire the night before; they were aware that they could be attacked at any moment by troops defending the Mobile & Ohio Railroad. To protect their small column from ambush, scouts were sent ahead while others trailed behind. Extra flankers were sent off the road hundreds of yards into the woods on both left and right. Attacked from any direction, the detachment would have time to orient and defend itself.

After finding the Second Iowa and passing Colonel Grierson's orders on to Colonel Hatch, the third detachment turned back to Sloan's plantation. The Iowans rode off toward Chesterville to make their feint at an encampment there.

With much of the brigade scattered across the hostile countryside, Grierson subdivided his command again. He rode south with the Sixth toward the town of Pontotoc, ordering Colonel Prince to follow with the Seventh when the diversionary companies returned. Following was difficult. The rain had stopped, but the Pontotoc road had become a gummy marsh of clay, churned by thousands of preceding hooves. Rid-

A detachment of cavalry from the Third Indiana Regiment. The unit's officer is seated, third from left, in a field chair while troopers sit on ammunition boxes.
LIBRARY OF CONGRESS

ers struggled to maintain a line as their horses sank in mud and ruts. They knew that a well-planned ambush would catch them nearly helpless to maneuver. Mounting tension may have made several troopers overreact that afternoon.

When the Seventh stopped at a farmhouse to water and feed the mounts, an unofficial search party found a keg of gunpowder and a number of antique U.S. Army muskets hidden. Without consulting an officer, the searchers set the farmhouse ablaze. It was official policy to burn enemy buildings warehousing guns and ammunition, but it was foolhardy to draw attention to themselves. Seeing the blaze, Colonel Prince organized a fire-fighting party that fought a losing battle, and the house burned completely. Afterward "the officers made every effort to find the guilty party, but it occurred mysteriously, no one knew anything about it," wrote Sergeant Surby. Prince was probably as alarmed by the useless destruction of property as by the possibility of discovery. Determining what was fair game in hostile territory, and what wasn't, was a constant struggle for officers and men of both armies.

The Federal guidelines for operating behind enemy lines were written by Henry Halleck, commanding general of the U.S. Army. He said that living off the enemy population's goods was proper if "regulated to repress pillage and . . . levied with fairness and moderation." Pillage was defined as "goods taken by force from an enemy" and as "wholesale robbery or destruction"; it could be either. It was also proper to confiscate or destroy any property that would help the enemy's war efforts.

In most cases, the boundaries separating pillage from theft were clear. A herd of Thoroughbred horses had military value, but a hay barn did not. Rifles hidden in a civilian's home should be confiscated, but not the homeowner's silverware and furniture. But even legitimate confiscation disturbed many soldiers; it seemed like theft. More than fifty years later, Henry Eby, a member of Grierson's brigade, wrote, "I often felt grieved for people in the South, when their stock, grain and fences were appropriated for the use of the army."

As the war stretched from months to years, maintaining discipline among frustrated, homesick soldiers became harder. In some soldiers' minds, every civilian who had not surrendered was part of the war effort; they were all fair game. Confiscation often graduated to looting. Sergeant Stephen Forbes was sickened by this scene: "The column halted for a few moments in front of the dwelling of a poor widow said by all her neighbors to be loyal to our cause, and immediately her yard and house were filled by a crowd of thieves (I cannot call them soldiers, for shame) who instantly appropriated everything they could carry. Some attacked her poultry, chasing the chickens and geese through her very house, and stones and clubs flew in all directions. Others butchered her hogs and splitting them in two, buckled them on their saddles, still warm and dripping with blood. Others took fence rails and burst in the doors of her smokehouse and granary, and in a few moments every morsel of sustenance which a hard year's work had brought her had disappeared as if before a pack of ravening wolves. The poor lone woman wrung her hands and cried in an agony of despair and terror, and prayed to God to help her, while her children sobbed and screamed in a perfect frenzy of fear. A soldier in rear of me said: 'I don't hardly like to see the boys go down on poor folks that way.' 'Damn them,' said I, so full of indignant rage that everything looked white. 'I wish that everyone of the wretches might be hung in chains and burned to death.' "

The wise nineteen-year-old sergeant could also see beyond his disgust: "Appropriating the last horse of a poor old woman, and driving off a man's team from before his plow, certainly seems to be tolerably small work for a soldier, but then what is all war but one monstrous evil by the use of which we hope to overcome a much greater, and so long as it tends to subdue the rebellion I suppose that the means are justified by the end."

Before Grierson's Mississippi raid, Federal armies moved fully supplied. A force of twenty thousand infantrymen traveled with dozens of food and ammunition supply wagons. Soldiers stole livestock to enliven their diets, but commanders like Grant and Sherman thoroughly disapproved of pillaging. They considered it unprofessional and often punished transgressors.

The raid helped change those rules. The raiders had to live off the land or starve. As Grierson remembered: "The three days cooked rations in haversacks . . . had all disappeared and we were living entirely off the country." Even taking from multiple plantations, "the command seldom got more than one good meal a day." For cavalry on the move, feeding horses was a greater problem than feeding men. Quartermaster General Montgomery Meigs's standing order was that "a horse requires nearly 26 pounds per day of food and a man but three pounds."

Because store shelves were barren, finding plantations every day with food for men and horses was imperative. Each day had to be filled with diversionary movements, steady southward progress, and a meal, if possible, at day's end. To accomplish that, Grierson was given an unsigned "intelligence report" before leaving La Grange. The report pinpointed locations of supposedly well stocked plantations and hidden livestock herds. It detailed the sites of Confederate warehouses,

The ruins of a factory near Richmond, Virginia. Because cameras were very rare, equipment was cumbersome, and photography was expensive in the 1860s, it is unlikely that a burned-out barn or warehouse was considered worth photographing. LIBRARY OF CONGRESS

enemy troop dispositions, road conditions, and more. Grierson had to rely on the report, accurate or not. Nearly seventeen hundred troopers were being guided through hostile country by a man whose only physical resources were an anonymous report, a pocket compass, a pocket map of Mississippi, and a Jew's harp—music was always essential to Grierson.

As the Sixth approached Pontotoc that afternoon, Grierson expected organized resistance. A charge by advance troops brought fire from armed citizens and a detachment of state troops. Seeing the size of Grierson's regiment, the soldiers wisely retreated and the locals fled for their homes—all save one. A lone Confederate soldier continued firing until he was shot and killed. Four miles north of Pontotoc, Prince heard the shots and charged the town to close ranks.

Meanwhile, a quick inspection by the Sixth uncovered a cache of ammunition and supplies hidden in the county courthouse. All was brought out into the street and destroyed, sparing the building. With nothing of importance there, Grierson and the Sixth led the vanguard south in search of a campsite. Left behind to search thoroughly, the Seventh discovered a warehouse filled with salt—a precious commodity. Before refrigeration was invented, salting or curing with salt was the principal way to keep meat from spoiling. The thousands of pounds destroyed near Pontotoc would eventually mean less preserved beef for Confederate soldiers.

Before nightfall, the three regiments were nearly reunited as they occupied two adjoining plantations selected by Grierson. Colonel Hatch and his Iowans arrived weary of being fired on. Mississippi state troops had skirmished with the Second Iowa through the night and all day Sunday. As Hatch's troops wheeled north, feinted toward Chesterville, and then headed southeast to rejoin the brigade, the Mississippi soldiers kept pace and distance. Firing from ambush, they pursued the Iowans for over eighteen hours before falling back.

Bedding down that night, the troopers were still in the dark about the mission's goal. Grierson knew that they had gone seventy miles into Mississippi without death or serious injury; they had at least two hundred miles more of danger and uncertainty ahead.

Completing the mission was possible only if the Confederates fell for Grierson's diversionary tactics. So far, they had.

Lieutenant Colonel Clark Barteau's Second Tennessee Cavalry had taken the bait and ridden to reinforce the Chesterville camp. He posted pickets and directed the Mississippi volunteers training there to form a defensive line Sunday morning. His hopes for a fight with the Yankees were raised when scouts told him Hatch was approaching. But as night fell in Chesterville, Barteau was still waiting in vain for a cavalry column that had turned southeast hours earlier.

At 10 p.m., a scout arrived with news that the Federals had raided Pontotoc. His swift-moving opponent must have astonished Barteau—he had no way of knowing the size of Grierson's force or that regiments were operating separately. Guessing that the Okolona station on the Mobile & Ohio Railroad was the Federal target, Barteau pooled all the mounted troops available at Chesterville and marched at midnight.

A few hours earlier, news of Union raids reached Confederate headquarters in Jackson, Mississippi. General John C. Pemberton commanded the entire Mississippi theater of war. Until that evening, his major concern had been Grant's troop movements on the Mississippi River threatening all-important Vicksburg. Reports of several troop movements across the Tennessee border could represent a serious threat or merely a demonstration, a ruse. Either way, Pemberton wanted help. In a telegram to his superior, General Joseph E. Johnston, he concluded, "The enemy are endeavoring to compel a diversion of my troops to Northern Mississippi."

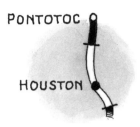

PONTOTOC

HOUSTON

DAY FOUR: MONDAY, APRIL 20

Shortly after 2 a.m., buglers blew the reveille call in Grierson's camp. Within moments, close to seventeen hundred men were in motion: rolling and packing bedding, combing the grounds for firewood, feeding horses, making breakfast. The morning's meal would be no more than coffee—Union soldiers drank quarts of coffee every day, if they had time to boil it over open fires in round tin pots—and hardtack.

Hardtack was a flour-and-water cracker. Each was roughly three inches wide, two inches long, and a half-inch thick; twelve hardtack made a daily bread ration. Called everything from "teeth dullers" to "sheet-iron," they had to be soaked before chewing. Often, hardtack was infested with worms or weevils: "It was no uncommon occurrence for a man to find the surface of his pot of coffee swimming with weevils after breaking up hardtack in it," one Federal infantryman wrote, "but they were easily skimmed off and left no distinctive flavor behind." It is no wonder that soldiers looked to the enemy's cattle and poultry for nourishment.

A second flurry of activity spread through camp as company sergeants yelled out the command "Prepare for inspection!"

Troopers maneuvered their horses into position and stood at attention, long rows of men and horses facing forward in the predawn light. Company commanders then closely surveyed each man and animal, picking individual troopers and horses to fall out. All those chosen were ailing—men with malarial fever or dysentery and horses that were lamed or weak. The men rightly assumed that they were being sent back to La Grange.

"I gave orders," Grierson recalled, "to the regimental commanders to cause a close inspection [of] regiments to be made with a view of selecting therefrom all men and horses any way disabled or not fit for further hard marching . . . thus freeing the command of any incumbrance . . . When the detachments were brought together I personally inspected every man as to his fitness for further active duty." Many men pleaded to stay with the brigade. Grierson exempted those who "were of the right kind of stuff to recuperate."

Soldiers care for a general's horses in rural Virginia. Cavalry officers and troopers changed mounts too frequently to become attached to their horses.
LIBRARY OF CONGRESS

As the "less effectives" formed up for the return march, their comrades instantly dubbed them the "Quinine Brigade." All Civil War soldiers were familiar with quinine, the standard treatment for malaria. Before the war's end, one of every four Federal soldiers was treated for symptoms of malaria. And malaria was not even the most common illness of soldiers. In this era before immunization and antibiotics, epidemic waves swept through the camps of both armies. There were massive outbreaks of smallpox and measles. Large numbers fell to yellow fever and typhoid. Pneumonia and tuberculosis were common. Forty-seven thousand men in the Federal army contracted scurvy, even though officials knew eating citrus fruit prevented it. Providing citrus fruit to the army was nearly impossible. Dysentery, looseness of the bowels, killed more than fifty-seven thousand soldiers in the Federal army alone. Tragically, more than four soldiers in the Union army died from sickness for every soldier who died on the battlefield; Confederate army losses were as bad.

Contagious diseases were worst among units from the agricultural western states. Men raised in crowded cities had been exposed to childhood diseases like measles and mumps and were more likely to be immune to them. Men who had grown up on frontier farms, relatively isolated from people, fell prey more easily to contagious diseases of all kinds. Many afflictions affected the men equally. Poor diet caused scurvy, inadequate clothing and shelter promoted colds and pneumonia, and primitive sanitation conditions made diarrhea and dysentery widespread in army camps.

Nobody was disease-proof, certainly not doctors. They were seven times more likely to die from disease than from battlefield injuries. Of course, there were not nearly enough doctors available in the army. Grierson's brigade, by regulation, should have had at least three surgeons; it had one. And he could not be spared to tend to the Quinine Brigade.

Returning the "less effectives" was compassionate *and* strategic. They were decoys, camouflage for the brigade's southward movements. Grierson explained the trick to his command in this dispatch, penciled in the dim light of a wood fire:

HEADQUARTERS FIRST CAVALRY BRIGADE
Five Miles south of Pontotoc, April 20, 1863.

GENERAL: At 3 a.m. I send an expedition, composed of the less effective portion of the command, to return by the most direct route to La Grange. Major Love, selected to take command, will hand you this. They pass through Pontotoc in the night, marching by fours, obliterating our tracks, and producing the impression that we have all returned . . .

I start at 4 o'clock in the morning, and on the night of the 20th shall be 50 miles below here. Everything looks exceedingly favorable. Rest assured that I shall spare no exertion to make the expedition as effective as possible. I may possibly find an opportunity to communicate with you again in four or five days, but do not wonder if you should not hear from me in thirty days.

We have yet encountered no force except the unorganized cavalry scattered through the country. We have succeeded in killing 4 or 5, and wounding and capturing a number. The prisoners return with this expedition.

Respectfully, your obedient servant,

B. H. GRIERSON, Colonel, Commanding Cavalry Brigade

Grierson also gave Major Hiram Love this letter for his wife, Alice Grierson:

My dear Alice,

I am sending back from this point about 200 men, the less effective portion of my command; sick, and those inclined to be sick; prisoners, led horses, mules, &c. . . . All is well, and everything looks favorable. We have had considerable skirmishing with the rebels; killed and wounded a number, and captured about 25. No loss on our side, and no one injured. May have an opportunity of writing again in a week or two; if not, do not be uneasy. I still have faith *and hope that all will be well. The column will move at 3 o'clock; want to march over 40 miles before night. This will be mailed to you at La Grange. I want to get one hour's sleep, if possible, before starting. Love to all. Hastily, but truly and affectionately, BHG.*

The Quinine Brigade marched north to Pontotoc on schedule. Riding by fours, they left behind convincing evidence— the raiders had returned north. Minutes later, the reduced brigade filed out of camp, one regiment at a time, taking the road south straight to Houston, Mississippi.

At the same time, Lieutenant Colonel Barteau was urging his troops forward at breakneck pace. With nearly eight hundred men and three artillery pieces, Barteau could give the Yankees a real fight when he caught them. He would have caught them if he had simply followed the trail left by Hatch's retreat from Chesterville.

By eight that morning, Barteau's scouts had found no trace of the raiders' heading toward the Mobile & Ohio Railroad.

Unsure of his next move, Barteau called an officers' council, which decided to backtrack to Pontotoc. Less than two hours on, advance scouts rode back from Pontotoc with news that the raiders had passed through that town during the night. The Federals were retreating northwest, toward Oxford; Barteau followed. Colonel Grierson would have relished knowing his trick had worked—the Confederates were hurriedly pursuing the Quinine Brigade.

Had he known, Grierson would have realized that he had not achieved a victory; the raiders merely gained a temporary advantage. The raid was akin to a real-life board game. Barteau's men had not been taken off the board; they had been sent back a move. Years later, Stephen Forbes captured the nature of the perilous game he had played in 1863: "A cavalry raid at its best is essentially a *game* of strategy and speed, with personal violence as an incidental complication. It is played according to more or less definite rules, not inconsistent, indeed, with the players' killing each other if the game cannot be won in any other way; but it is commonly a strenuous game, rather than a bloody one, intensely exciting, but not necessarily very dangerous." But keeping danger at a minimum required creating maximum confusion—Grierson's primary tactic.

That afternoon a small advance party of the Second Iowa galloped into Houston to make as much noise as possible and capture the town's complete attention. The rest of the raiders had left the main road and surreptitiously bypassed the town. It was just another dreary day's work for most of the raiders. "The day being cloudy and damp, there was little interest displayed in viewing the country," Sergeant Surby's journal reveals. Surby realized that the troopers, after leaving the road, were "making a new one through a wheat field of some extent;

it was about six inches in height and of a beautiful green, which was a change from the mud." Few of the raiders appreciated how much the Mississippi landscape had changed after two years of war.

In 1861, all the fields in that area would have been sown with cotton; "King Cotton" was *the* crop of the Deep South. When eleven Southern states seceded from the Union, they had the manpower to create an army that rivaled the United States Army. But the Confederate States of America was unable to build a navy to challenge the Union's navy. There were no factories in the South to turn out steel, no shipyards to build in, not enough skilled workers. Blockading Confederate ports was easy work for the Federals. The South could not ship cotton to European buyers; raw cotton clogged warehouses and storage barns throughout the South. And food was desperately needed for the army and northern states of the Confederacy. Mississippi was transformed from the "Cotton Kingdom" to endless fields of wheat.

Eventually the brigade returned to the main road and stopped at a plantation south of Houston. The troopers had traveled forty miles that day, as Grierson predicted before the dawn. Finding a well-stocked plantation as planned proved the accuracy of both Grierson's navigation and his anonymous intelligence report.

Colonel Grierson knew exactly where he was that night. Others, though, were stymied. General Stephen Hurlbut, Grierson's superior stationed in Memphis, was absolutely uninformed. Still, he did not hesitate to send a glowing report to General Grant's headquarters: "My cavalry from La Grange have before this destroyed the railroad below and near Tupelo, and in the confusion may get fairly started across Alabama before they are known." Of course, the raiders had made no assault on the Mobile & Ohio and were not heading toward Alabama. Hurlbut went on to assure Grant that "Grierson will cut the railroad, if he lives . . . about Wednesday night or Thursday."

Misinformation abounded in the Confederate camps, too. General Ruggles, commander of the eastern Mississippi defenses, knew what had nearly happened at his Chesterville camp but could not guess the raiders' current location. His Second Alabama Cavalry telegraphed hard information: six thousand Northern cavalrymen were seen heading toward Houston. Ruggles refused to believe that that many Yankees had slipped past his patrols. He then got a remarkably accu-

rate report from an officer at Okolona: "Reliable scout reports enemy about 2,000 strong, with five mounted howitzers, on Houston road . . . Negroes report hearing them say they were going to the Southern road [the Vicksburg Railroad] or Grenada."

When this message was telegraphed to General Pemberton in Jackson, it left no room for doubt—a substantial and dangerous Federal cavalry troop was loose in northern Mississippi. It had to be stopped, destroyed, or captured before it did any serious damage.

Grant's plan was working. Pemberton's attention, so firmly focused on the defense of Vicksburg days before, had been split.

When Barteau finally made camp that night, his unit was frustrated and weary. The soldiers had traveled seventy miles since midnight—more than twice a normal day's march. And they had never even caught sight of the raiders. Barteau spent hours in Pontotoc as scouts scoured the countryside for information. By the time he confirmed that fewer than two hundred troopers—about two companies—were retreating north, he was far behind Grierson. A forced march brought Barteau's soldiers to Houston, where he wisely called a halt. All good cavalry commanders knew that men could work indefinitely without food, water, or rest; horses could not.

On the fourth day of the raid, General Stephen A. Hurlbut in Memphis had no news from Grierson. That did not prevent him from forwarding a glowing report to General Grant. LIBRARY OF CONGRESS

STARKVILLE   PALO ALTO

DAY FIVE: TUESDAY, APRIL 21

★ As troopers of the Sixth and Seventh dried their wet clothing over smoky cook fires early Tuesday morning, they were sure something big was in the works. The Second Iowa had prepared to march hours before dawn.

Concern had spread through the camp Monday night. Sergeant Surby remembered "the prevailing opinion was, that the enemy was near at hand." And whatever the raiders' ultimate mission was, they had not accomplished it yet. They had not "played smash" with any railroad; they hadn't even tried. How many men observed Grierson and his senior officers meeting together hour after hour that night?

Grierson had bared the facts: the brigade was already deep into enemy territory with a very long ride still ahead; a large force, Barteau's, was in pursuit behind; more opposition forces had to be forming in front and on their flanks; a collision with any sizable enemy would wreck their chance of reaching the Vicksburg Railroad. All the officers agreed that a convincing demonstration was called for, a demonstration that would permanently divide the brigade into two separate forces moving in opposite directions. Colonel Hatch's Second Iowa was chosen to be the decoy.

Grierson elected to cut the Iowans loose from the main column because their horses were the least healthy and he was more familiar with the officers of the Illinois regiments. But the Iowans had the best chance of surviving alone because they were the best-armed regiment he commanded. All three regiments carried weapons made by a number of civilian manufacturers: Burnside, Cosmopolitan, Starr, Smith, Sharp, Colt, and others. Some models loaded and fired more quickly than others. Some models were more accurate than others. The Second Iowa was well stocked with two superior models, the Sharp's carbine and the Colt revolving rifle.

The Sharp's was light at eight and a half pounds and reasonably accurate. It had a unique firing mechanism that allowed troopers to fire and reload nearly four times faster than with other carbines. The Colt rifle was much longer than a carbine, difficult to fire from horseback and time-consuming to load. But it fired six shots without reloading and was highly accurate at long range.

No Confederate units possessed equivalent firepower. In a pitched battle against rebels armed with single-shot, low-accuracy rifles and shotguns, the Iowans had a powerful advantage. Grierson knew that they could shoot their way out of trouble. With that in mind, his orders to Hatch were incredibly ambitious: "Proceed to the Mobile and Ohio Railroad in the vicinity of West Point [Mississippi], and destroy the road and wires; thence move south, destroying the railroad and all public property as far south, if possible, as Macon; thence across the railroad, making a circuit northward; if practicable, take Columbus and destroy all Government works in that place, and again strike the railroad south of Okolona, and, destroying it, return to La Grange by the most practicable route."

At 7 a.m., the brigade commenced operations. All three regiments marched south; the Iowans took the rear. At a pre-arranged spot on the road to Starkville, most of the Iowans were halted while one company of troopers with a mule-drawn Woodruff gun followed the main column. After riding more than a quarter mile, they reversed to cover their tracks.

Colonel Hatch may or may not have been grateful to have the two-pounder cannon with him. The gun's carriage was make-shift and often broke. The shell it fired was light and its range was short compared with Confederate field weapons. Ranking Union generals were reluctant to buy the weapon and only thirty were placed with Illinois and Iowa regiments in 1861. The combat effectiveness of the Woodruff gun was still unproved in 1863.

"This patrol returned in columns of fours, thus obliterating all the outward bound tracks. The cannon was turned in the road in four different places, thus making their tracks correspond with the four pieces of artillery which Grierson had with the expedition. The object of this was to deceive the rebels, who were following us, into the belief that the entire column had taken the Columbus road," wrote Sergeant Lyman Pierce of the Second Iowa.

And it worked like a charm. The dogged Barteau found the raiders' abandoned campsite a few hours later and sent scouts galloping off for information. Barteau's scouts encountered Hatch's rear guard minutes later. When they retreated to inform Barteau, he was already at the Starkville road reading the tracks in the clay. Two days earlier, Barteau had guessed wrong at Chesterville and allowed Hatch to escape unharmed. The day before, he had refused to be tricked by the retreat of the Quinine Brigade. Looking at the hoofprints of horses moving in fours with four artillery pieces trailing behind, Barteau convinced himself that the main Yankee force had turned toward Columbus to attack the Mobile & Ohio Railroad. He realized that some of Grierson's force, probably making a feint before retreating, had gone south, but the Mobile & Ohio had to be the Federals' target. There was no target to the south that the Yankees could possibly reach. Barteau scribbled this entry in the report he was keeping for General Ruggles: "The enemy had divided, 200 going to Starkville and 700 continuing their march on the West Point [rail]road." The "200" going to Starkville were actually more than 950 men still under Grierson's command.

The roads were treacherously sloppy—it had rained for hours—but Barteau drove his men hastily forward. Near the village of Palo Alto, shots rang out and Barteau ordered his command to gallop. At the top of a rise in the road, Barteau looked down on a pleasing scene. His troops were surrounding the rear-guard pickets of Hatch's regiment. Overpowered, the pickets surrendered and dropped their weapons. Farther ahead, the main body of Hatch's regiment was riding into a long, narrow lane bounded by a rail fence overgrown with brush on one side and by a thick row of hedges on the other.

Most troopers in Grierson's brigade carried cavalry carbines made by a number of different manufacturers. They were relatively short, lightweight single-shot rifles with limited accuracy. From the top: Sharp's, Smith, Cosmopolitan, Burnside, and Starr. Many Second Iowa troopers carried a Colt revolving rifle, at bottom, which could fire six shots without reloading and was more accurate than a carbine. WEST POINT MUSEUM

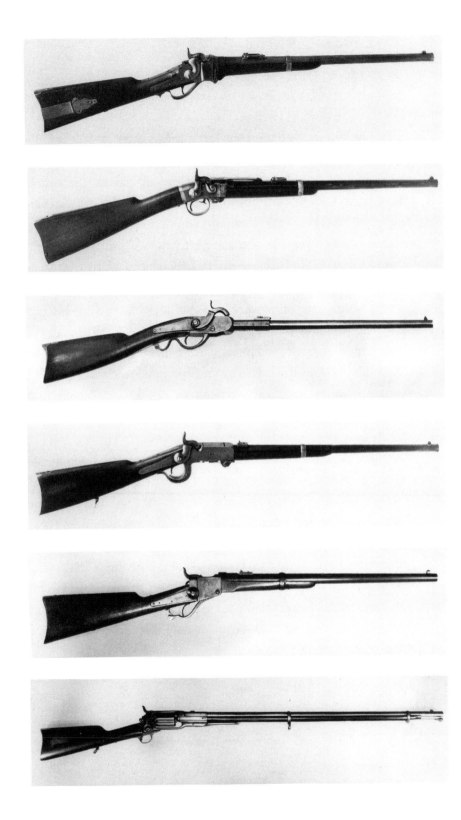

A church and stand of trees were at the end of the lane to Hatch's front.

The raiders were boxed in. Barteau had them.

Hatch's Iowans dismounted immediately. Horse-holders (every fourth rider) took charge of the animals as the rest of the troopers took cover and fired at the Confederates. Barteau called a halt and issued orders: four companies of his Tennessee regulars were sent dashing to the far end of the lane, Hatch's front. The rest, with the Mississippi state troops he had commandeered in Chesterville, would hold the rear.

Two hours later, they were at a standoff. Hatch kept his regiment in the lane. Barteau realigned his troops, putting all the Mississippi troopers at Hatch's front, protected by the cover of woods and the church. Dismounted there, they were told to hold fire unless the Iowans tried to break out. Meanwhile, Barteau formed all his Tennessee cavalry to Hatch's rear for a mounted charge into the lane.

Before Barteau could execute the plan, Hatch opened fire with his mounted Woodruff gun. The barrage of cannon shell alarmed the inexperienced Mississippi state soldiers. Colonel Hatch commented later that his Confederate opponent "may have underestimated the frightening effects of the two-pounder cannon," just as Union leaders had underestimated the weapon two years earlier. When the vanguard of Hatch's regiment burst forward and fell upon the Mississippians, they broke and "retreated in the utmost disorder," according to one Confederate officer.

Barteau, a veteran of several bloody battles, forgot what "seeing the elephant" was like. Young men joining the army were eager to "see the elephant," to experience the larger-than-life excitement and challenge of battle. They yearned to prove their manhood under fire, but the Mississippians couldn't have known what to expect that day. They were very recent recruits, still in training, hardly ready to withstand the fury of combat-hardened veterans running, screaming, firing time and again at their heads. Military psychologists say combat is always a surprise and a shock, because there is no way of preparing for the emotional impact short of actual experience. The shock of combat sent half of Barteau's force reeling.

Sergeant Pierce described the engagement from the Iowans' point of view:

> *Company H was on picket. They gallantly repulsed the first charge made by the rebels, and aided by Company E held the enemy in check until Hatch could form a line . . . where his men, being covered by the trees, could command with their rifles the open field in their front, across which the enemy must advance. Our little cannon was placed in a favorable position, and did good service . . .*
>
> *Our boys kept the cover of the trees until they were within short range, when they opened upon them such a murderous fire from their trusty revolving rifles that they were not only repulsed, but stampeded and scattered all over the wood. The rebels acknowledged a loss of twenty-five in this skirmish, and citizens said their loss was much heavier. Owing to the completeness of our cover not a drop of Yankee blood was shed.*

The Confederates' disorder was so complete that, fleeing in retreat, they abandoned the party of Iowa troopers captured hours earlier.

Taking the advantage, Hatch pushed the ragged Mississippians forward toward the railroad. Barteau's Tennessee cavalry looped around, finally getting behind his retreating Mississippi state troops. By nightfall, the skirmishing had ended with Barteau's troops forming a barrier between Hatch and the railroad junction. Sending out couriers for reinforcements, Barteau was convinced that the next morning would bring a conclusive battle—the Federals had to go through Barteau to reach the Mobile & Ohio.

Colonel Hatch had no intention of challenging Barteau a second time, though. The Iowa regiment moved northward before the dawn; Barteau's force followed. "Believing it was

The horrifying aspects of close-quarters combat. Raw recruits were always eager to experience the thrill of battle, to "see the elephant" for the first time. But none could fully imagine the terrifying sights and sounds of warfare beforehand.
HARPER'S WEEKLY

important to divert the enemy's cavalry from Colonel Grier-son," Hatch later reported, "I moved slowly northward, fight-ing by the rear, crossing the Houlka River, and drawing their forces immediately in my rear." Yet again Grierson's strategy had worked.

The colonel had addressed another need at a brigade staff meeting the night before: "As we approached the heart of the rebel country I felt the need of a larger and more effective force of scouts . . . The duty was so hazardous and the dif-ficulties so great . . . that the service had necessarily to be voluntary." Grierson proposed a group of scouts who would travel far ahead of the raiders, inconspicuous scouts who would talk freely with Southern citizens and Confederate sol-diers and learn vital secrets. Grierson wanted spies—confident, quick-witted men who could mingle among the enemy and not arouse suspicion. Masquerading in Confederate uniforms, they would certainly be shot if captured.

Lieutenant Colonel William Blackburn of the Seventh Illi-nois claimed he had the right men; his quartermaster sergeant, Richard Surby, should lead them. A quartermaster was respon-sible for providing living quarters for the troopers, laying out the camp, and looking after the rations, ammunition, and other supplies. Quartermasters, commissary officers, and the like supported the fighting troops; as a rule, support personnel did not fight. They were sarcastically called "bulletproof" for obvious reasons.

A Canadian immigrant who worked on the railroads prior to the war, Surby loved adventure and the outdoors life. He also loved writing. Sergeant Surby kept a detailed journal of his service throughout the war, although "it was written under the most embarrassing circumstances; just imagine yourself trying to write in an army tent, with six jolly comrades . . . talking and laughing on various subjects."

He jumped at the opportunity to form a team of scouts: "This suited me, and without hesitation I accepted the position with thanks, fully resolved not to abuse the confidence reposed in me. I received orders to take six or eight men, proceed at once on the advance and procure citizens['] dress, saddles, shot guns and everything necessary for our disguise. It did not take long to do this, and by noon reported myself and men ready for duty."

Finding citizens' dress was no problem; the scouts simply searched every farmhouse near the road to Starkville and confiscated the clothing, and weapons, they needed. And they didn't have to be too particular. Any hat, shirt, or pair of pants that was not Union blue could be part of a Confederate uniform. When the Civil War began, nearly 90 percent of all American factories were located in Northern states. Just as the South lacked gun factories and shipbuilding yards, it also lacked clothing mills to make uniforms from its abundant crops of cotton. "We have no cities. We don't want them . . . We want no manufactures . . . no mechanical or manufacturing classes. As long as we have our rice, our sugar, our tobacco, and our cotton, we can command wealth to purchase all we want," said one Alabama politician. But once war was declared, they could no longer buy what they wanted from the North.

Although gray was the Confederacy's official uniform color, very few soldiers were issued gray uniforms. The most common uniform color was butternut brown, achieved by dyeing clothing with walnut hulls. In practically no time, members of the scout unit had acquired enough odd pieces of butternut clothing to shed their factory-made blues and ride back

into the raiders' column dressed as Confederate "irregulars" or "guerrillas." The disguise worked; their fellow troopers mistook them for Confederate prisoners. Minutes later, they were dubbed the "Butternut Guerrillas," a name that stuck.

Given the "point," this advance guard's first mission was to precede the column into Starkville. If they found danger ahead, the Butternuts galloped back to warn the column. Otherwise, their job was to report the road conditions and the position of streams, bridges, and other important geographic features. The eight men divided near day's end to locate plantations with food and forage. Grierson hoped that the fast-moving Butternut Guerrillas could speed the march and give the raiders a precious time advantage. He wanted to stay "ahead of information," to reach a town before word was out that the raiders were coming.

As rain pelted them, Surby's guerrillas found Starkville's streets barren of activity; there were no enemy troops in sight. Some scouts stayed in town to see what more could be learned while the rest rode back to the column with the news that Starkville was clear. As the two regiments with 950 Federal troopers filed into town, the Butternuts took the point again and scouted southward.

Grierson's conversations with people in Starkville uncovered disturbing but expectable news: the raiders were not "ahead of information." The citizens had known that Federal troops were coming, just not so many. Grierson's mood must have been as vile as the weather that afternoon.

The daylong rain turned into a violent thunderstorm as the

Three Confederate troopers captured near Gettysburg in 1863. Because so many Confederates lacked regular uniforms, it was easy for the Butternut Guerrillas to pass for Southerners. LIBRARY OF CONGRESS

column struggled south. Filled by continuing rain, streams were overflowing. The road had turned into a muddy quagmire. For more than a mile, the troopers waded in water up to their horses' bellies. Finding some high ground, Grierson called a halt to the day's march. Men and horses weathered the storm roughly under dripping trees. The lucky ones found enough wood to make "mattresses." Several hundred—Major John Graham's First Battalion of the Seventh—got no rest at all and had no complaints about pulling night action. They could not get warm or dry in camp. On the move, they would be less annoyed by swarming mosquitoes.

Between Starkville and the campsite, Grierson had gotten a piece of intelligence, a tip, from a slave trying to run away from his masters and follow the raiders to freedom. Tips from slaves proved to be the most valuable information the raiders received. This man told Grierson that a large leather tannery and factory was off the main road only five miles away. Graham's battalion was ordered into the moonless gloom, through swamp and waist-high water, to find it.

The tannery was exactly where the cooperative slave had said it would be. After surrounding the wooden building, a platoon of Graham's men broke in and forced the surrender of a Confederate quartermaster sergeant and his civilian workmen. Graham had captured the first genuine prize of the raid. The factory was filled with boots, saddles, bridles, and other equipment, all labeled for shipment to the Confederate army at Vicksburg. Graham dispersed the workmen and left the building burning like a torch to light their way back to camp.

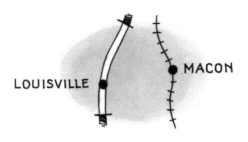

LOUISVILLE   MACON

DAY SIX: WEDNESDAY, APRIL 22

By this time, the raid had begun to inflict psychological strain on both sides: the raiders and the citizens of Mississippi. The raiders dreaded what ambush might lurk over each rise of the road. The locals, with rumors moving south faster than the raiders, dreaded destruction and death. Panic was bound to spread; townspeople were likely to come out shooting to protect themselves. A newspaper reported how insolently the Northerners treated Southern property, among which they included slaves:

> At Starkville they robbed the inhabitants of horses, mules, negroes, jewelry and money; went into the stores and threw their contents (principally tobacco) into the street or gave it to the negroes; caught the mail boy and took the mail, robbed the postoffice, but handed back a letter from a soldier to his wife, containing $50.00, and ordered the postmaster to give it to her ... Hale & Murdock's hat wagon, loaded with wool hats, passing through at the time was captured. They gave the hats to the negroes and took the mules. Starkville can boast of better head covering for its negroes than any other town in the state.

Grierson's official report noted only that his troopers confiscated and destroyed a quantity of "government property." It's impossible to know which report was more accurate, but it's unlikely that the troopers discarded tobacco. Tobacco, a Southern product in very short supply in the Federal army, was too valuable to give or throw away.

Grierson was interested in damage that morning: doing more damage to the Confederates and preventing them from reciprocating. He knew that telegraph messages had been sent from Starkville to all Confederate commanders the previous night. Certainly Pemberton, Ruggles, and Chalmers now knew that Hatch's movement toward West Point was a feint; the main column was going south. Unless Grierson could stage another believable demonstration at the Mobile & Ohio Railroad, the Confederates would concentrate on his front. They would mass troops between the raiders and the prized Vicksburg & Southern Railroad. Grierson needed two days to reach his destination. He needed one day's worth of distraction to make that possible. A force threatening the railroad at Macon, southeast of Starkville, would be the most convincing approach.

But Grierson could not throw off another large force like Hatch's Second Iowa. He could not spare as many as were in the Quinine Brigade. If the raiders had to fight the final miles to the Vicksburg Railroad, they needed all the manpower remaining.

The Sixth Illinois was already marching toward Louisville, the Seventh falling in behind, when Grierson asked Colonel Prince to spare his best company for a dangerous mission. Prince picked Company B without hesitation.

The men of Company B had served together since forming

in 1861. A powerful, almost-fatherly farmer, Captain Henry Forbes, had always been its leader. Two years of losses from death and disease had reduced the company to just forty men, one-third of full strength. But they were a close-knit group, tough fighters with "unit pride."

Prince relayed Grierson's orders: dash to the Macon railroad station, damage the railroad, cut the telegraph wires, attract as much attention as possible, and attempt to rejoin the Seventh regiment. Realizing how difficult the last task might be, Forbes asked, "What course will the brigade take after destroying the Vicksburg railroad?" Prince was uncertain. Grierson had no firm orders or certain plan. Prince suggested they might swing east into Alabama, then north to La Grange. Forbes's best bet was to complete the mission and catch up to the main column near Newton Station.

Captain Forbes called his company of forty to inspection and asked those too sick to ride day and night without rest to fall out. None did. Traveling down the line, the captain culled out five men. Company B, reduced to thirty-five troopers, rode hurriedly east—sometimes trotting, sometimes galloping—toward the rebel picket lines protecting the Macon junction. Both men and horses labored. The rain had finally stopped, but this bottomland district was still flooded and swampy.

Sergeant Surby, scouting ahead of Grierson's main column, summed up the mood, saying, "It was not known what force was at Macon, nor what force was following us." He was convinced that Company B was on a "perilous journey, and many feared that they would never see [Forbes] again." Sergeant Stephen Forbes, riding with his older brother and Company B, recalled that he imagined rejoining the Seventh in a Confederate prison camp. But whatever concerns the Federals had

for their safety were dwarfed by the growing civilian fears. Captain Forbes wrote: "We had not been long on our road [Starkville to Macon] before we were made aware of the ludicrous but tremendous panic which the raid was causing in these parts. As fast as men could ride and negroes run, the most exaggerated reports flew right and left, both as to the numbers and the conduct of our soldiers. Our hundreds became so many thousands, while our really restrained and considerate bearing towards the people was transmuted into every form of plunder and violence. The whole region was terrorized."

Captain Forbes found Mississippi life totally disrupted by the war:

The conscription had largely stripped the country of its natural defenders, yet there was a considerable contingent of white men to be found about the plantations. There were also many skulkers [draft dodgers] from the conscription and deserters from the confederate armies who were much more willing to shoot than to be shot. In every county and in most towns there were organizations of home guards, primarily raised to overawe the blacks and to keep in check the reckless elements of the population.

The women, the children, and the superannuated [elderly] men completed the list. This heterogeneous and not wholly normal populace was thrown into the wildest excitement as we sped through. Some wished to fight; many chose to run; and all

Lieutenant Colonel Henry C. Forbes of the Seventh Illinois in 1865. The older brother of Stephen Forbes, Henry Forbes was captain of Company B in the spring of 1863. HENRY CLINTON FORBES COLLECTION, ILLINOIS HISTORICAL SURVEY, UNIVERSITY OF ILLINOIS AT URBANA-CHAMPAIGN

busied themselves with attempts to secrete their property . . .
The negro men were sent away into the swamps with the stock
of all kinds, and oftentimes with wagon-loads of household stuff.
The white men, unless bearing arms, were generally secreted
from what was commonly supposed to be probable capture and
possible murder, in whatever best hiding-place could be devised;
while the women and children held the home against the
invader—and well indeed they did it. I never saw a southern
woman show undignified fear in her own home.

After a thirty-mile march, Company B halted that evening
to feed the horses at a plantation near Macon. Uncertain how
many troops were protecting the junction, Captain Forbes dispatched scouts, who quickly returned with a captured Confederate private. The rebel obligingly told Forbes that two
thousand infantrymen were expected that night by train to reinforce the railroad junction. Company B rested until train en-
gines were heard approaching Macon. Captain Forbes decided
a change of plans was required: "We thought it best to consider Macon too large a prize to be captured by thirty-six
men. Had we revealed our numbers by venturing among the
enemy, they would have swallowed us up as a half mouthful,
but as it was, they treated our Company with the most distin-
guished respect. Meanwhile we accomplished what we were
sent for; we kept all eyes on the Mobile & Ohio Railroad."

Company B's diversion was precious to the main column
of the raid. Flooding forced the regiments to zigzag between
road and marsh. The trip to Louisville was, Grierson wrote,
"twenty-eight miles mostly through a dense swamp . . . For
miles it was belly deep to the horses, in mud and mire so that
at times no road was discernible."

Finally reaching the outskirts of Louisville, Grierson sent an advance party to secure the town. They found it eerily empty—not a soul in sight. A quick reconnaissance showed that many residents, expecting the raiders, had boarded their windows and fled. "Those who remained at home . . . had expected to be robbed, outraged, and have their houses burned," Grierson learned. As the column marched through the ghost town, the troopers must have imagined hateful eyes, if not rifles, trained on them from behind curtained windows.

Grierson left Major Graham's First Battalion to guard the town until the column could get an hour's head start. "Let no one," Grierson ordered, "leave with information of the direction we have taken . . . preserve order, quiet the fears of these people." He also ordered two troopers to dress like civilians and make a run at the telegraph line along the Mobile & Ohio "to prevent information of our presence from flying along the railroad to Jackson." Company B might have been taken already, short of its goal.

"After leaving the town, we struck another swamp, in which, crossing it, as we were obliged to, in the dark, we lost several animals drowned, and the men narrowly escaped the same fate," Grierson reported. Colonel Prince reckoned the Seventh alone had lost twenty horses. Men who were able to save their saddles piled them on led horses—horses too lame or weak to be ridden. Ten miles south of Louisville, the column found dry ground on a plantation. Grierson had made the most of Company B's covering run; the column had traveled more than fifty miles under near-impossible conditions. The target, the Vicksburg Railroad, was little more than a day's ride away.

Compared with Captain Forbes and Colonel Grierson, Colonel Hatch had the most militarily profitable day on

April 22, his birthday. After the Iowa regiment's daylong encounter with Barteau at Palo Alto, it retreated off the main
roads. Sergeant Pierce remembered: "We soon entered a large
swamp through which we traveled by an obscure path, guided
by a negro until we struck the river . . . Here Hatch found
some flood-wood lodged against a fallen tree; with this he
constructed a rude foot-bridge, and we unsaddled our horses
and each trooper carried his saddle across the bridge on his
back. The bank on the side from which the horses must enter
was about six feet above the stream and very nearly perpendicular. Three or four troopers would seize each horse and
throw him into the stream, when they would, by the aid of
long poles, compel him to swim to the opposite bank, where
two men stood hip deep in water to aid him up the bank. In
this way the entire command was crossed in safety, between
the hours of 10 o'clock p.m. and 3 o'clock a.m., of as dark a
night as I ever experienced. Large bonfires were built on each
bank to expel the darkness. The cannon was taken to pieces
and hauled across by means of a rope. As soon as the column
was all over, we saddled up and moved out."

Their progress never challenged by Barteau, the Iowans
reached Okolona late in the day: "We charged into the town
just before sunset, where we burned thirty barracks filled with
Confederate British-stamped cotton [presumably cotton baled
and approved for export to the United Kingdom]. This done
we moved five miles out of town and camped for the night on
a wealthy plantation, which afforded everything we needed
both for animals and men."

Lieutenant Colonel Barteau had been less fortunate in
choosing a guide that day. The slave "helping" the Confederate
colonel got thoroughly lost in the same swampland. Barteau's

force ended the day nearly ten miles from Okolona with no hope of catching Hatch.

In Jackson, the news that reached General Pemberton was alarming. Dozens of reports and rumors flooded in, most contradicting each other. Pemberton was convinced that the Federal force invading Mississippi had fewer than two thousand men, but he could not determine their whereabouts. According to eyewitnesses, the main force was moving through Starkville and had just fought a battle in Palo Alto. Then Pemberton read that a large force was advancing on Macon; he was certain the raiders had turned east from Starkville. Of course, the large force was only Captain Forbes and Company B.

That night, Pemberton ordered countermeasures—actions to secure the defense of Vicksburg. First, he appointed General William Loring to take command temporarily of all Confederate troops north of Meridian, superseding General Ruggles. To give Loring a numerical advantage, he diverted an Alabama infantry brigade away from Vicksburg to join in the hunt for the Federals. That brigade was on the trains Captain Forbes heard pull into Macon.

General Pemberton may have overreacted because of the mounting citizen panic; he was sure to be blamed for it. Pemberton was widely distrusted and disliked in Mississippi because he was a Pennsylvania Yankee by birth. But being on the "wrong side" in the American Civil War was not too unusual.

Eleven Southern states seceded to form the Confederate States of America after the election of President Abraham Lincoln. After the call to war, men chose sides—Union or Confederate—for a host of reasons. State loyalty was not paramount. In border states like Kentucky and Missouri, it was common for brothers and fathers and sons to join different sides. Lieutenant Colonel Barteau had grown up in Ohio but became an ardent anti-abolitionist while living in Tennessee. He fought against his own brother at the Battle of Shiloh. Josiah Gorgas built all the new Southern factories turning out gunpowder and shells; he was a West Point graduate from Pennsylvania. On the Union side, Admiral David Farragut, the conqueror of New Orleans, was a Tennessee native who made his home in Virginia. Grierson's commander, Stephen Hurlbut, hailed from North Carolina.

C.S.A. General John C. Pemberton, commander of the Department of Mississippi at Jackson. A Pennsylvanian who married a Virginian, he resigned from the U.S. Army in 1861 to fight for his adopted homeland. LIBRARY OF CONGRESS

There was another reason for Pemberton's distraction. General Grant's planning had counted on it. As a young lieutenant, Grant had served with Pemberton in the Mexican War of 1846–1848. Grant had mentally filed away character flaws he saw in Pemberton then and was using Grierson to exploit those flaws.

Pemberton needed order. He was inflexible and uncommunicative. He disliked adjusting tactics to fit the situation before him. An army engineer, Pemberton preferred defending to attacking. He liked to mass his troops behind impenetrable fortifications, like Vicksburg's, and keep the enemy in front of him. Open-field operations confused him, and Grant knew it. In 1862, Pemberton was relieved of command in South Carolina because the public had no faith in his abilities. The state's governor complained that "Pemberton seems confused and uncertain about everything." Grant was confident that Grierson's mischief making would upset Pemberton and cloud his judgment. It was already beginning to work.

Late that night, Pemberton implored his commanding officer, General Joseph E. Johnston, for aid: "Heavy raids are making from Tennessee deep into the State . . . Could you not make a demonstration with a cavalry force in their rear?" What could a cavalry raid from hundreds of miles away accomplish? No help from Johnston could stop Grierson now.

DAY SEVEN: THURSDAY, APRIL 23

The Butternut Guerrillas were invaluable. Operating miles ahead of the main column, they were Grierson's eyes and ears. And they did more than provide safe passage for the brigade; they also found fresh mounts. Sergeant Surby quickly realized that getting information "was quite easy in our assumed characters, when conversing with . . . hunters we passed ourselves off as confederates . . . ordered to keep in advance of the Yankees, watch their movements and . . . report to the nearest post . . . We obtained their confidence, and was told where they had concealed their fine animals."

Their disguises and adopted Southern accents were accepted without question. They were startled by two genuine Confederate soldiers at one farmhouse they visited. After greetings were exchanged and a bottle of "old rye" whiskey was passed around, Surby warned the Confederates that Yankee invaders were coming. The Confederates fled with their new comrades: "We started out, the young men armed with shotguns, eight negroes following with fourteen mules and six fine horses. It was about one and a half miles to the road, upon which the column was advancing, and in the direction that we were going; when about half way I had a curiosity to examine their guns, which they seemed proud to exhibit; making a motion to one of my men he followed suit, thus we had them disarmed." It seemed a fine joke until they saw the Federals' main column and realized that they were prisoners.

Unintentionally, the entire brigade of blue-coated troopers passed for Confederates. After days of riding and wading through mud, their uniforms were thoroughly caked with a mix of red clay and gray sand. When the raiders passed a tiny country schoolhouse, the teacher mistook them for Confederate cavalry and called a recess for the children. "They flocked to the roadside, hurrahing for Beauregard, Van Dorn, and the Confederacy. One little girl thought she recognized one of the men and running up asked . . . if her uncle was along," Grierson recalled in his *Record of Services Rendered the Government, 1863*. "The men were so covered with mud or dust, that at a distance they might pass for gray, and when the blue was perceived, it was supposed to be *captured* clothing, which it seems the rebels not unusually wore."

On the raid's seventh morning, the scouts had a specific tactical mission: capture and hold a bridge. The weather was cloudy and dry, but the low-lying countryside was flooded from days of rain; rivers overflowed their banks. Grierson's map showed a bridge over the Pearl River that had to be crossed later. He did not want Confederates to burn it as a delaying tactic. Surby received unambiguous orders: "My object was to save life if possible, the bridge at all hazards."

The scouts traveled uneventfully through the sparsely farmed countryside until they spotted an elderly man on a mule two miles from the bridge. Surby approached alone: "We passed the time of day and entered into conversation. The old man informed me that a picket was stationed at the bridge, composed of citizens, numbering five in all, his son being one of the party; all were armed with shotguns. They had torn up several planks from the center of the bridge, and had placed combustibles on it ready to ignite at our approach."

Some time after the other scouts joined the conversation, the man became suspicious. "Gentlemen, gentlemen, you are not what you seem to be, you certainly are Yankees." Surby tried to frighten the man to gain his cooperation: "It lies in your power to save your buildings from the torch, to save your own life, and probably that of your son, by saving the bridge." The threat worked. The old man accompanied the scouts to the Pearl River bridge; he would tell the defenders to surrender. Concealed by undergrowth, Surby watched this scene unfold: "When within a dozen yards of the bridge, he halted, and commenced telling his errand; but ere he had hardly half through, I could perceive some signs of uneasiness on the side of his listeners, they all at once jumped upon their horses and away they went. We then advanced to the bridge, replaced the planks, found two shot guns, that they had left in their flight, and leaving one man to wait for the column and turn the old man over to the Colonel, I proceeded with the rest to Philadelphia, [Mississippi]."

Surby observed that Colonel Grierson had been right on both counts that morning. First, word of the raiders was racing ahead of them; the bridge was defended and ready for burning. Second, the river could not be forded; the current was too fast for horses to swim across.

Danger signs were everywhere now. The bridge defenders, retreating to the town of Philadelphia, raised the alarm as they traveled. Every farm the scouts passed was deserted. Occa-

Harper's Weekly *presented a thrilling battle for the Pearl River bridge that never occurred. Warned that Union troops were approaching, Confederate defenders abandoned the bridge without firing a shot.* FRANK AND MARIE-THERESE WOOD PRINT COLLECTIONS

sionally they spied groups of armed riders ahead galloping toward the town. As the scouts approached Philadelphia, Surby saw armed men waiting in the main street and reacted: "I immediately sent a man back, requesting the commanding officer of the advance guard to send me ten men. I waited long enough to see they were coming, and turning to my men ordered them to charge, and as we neared them [the townsmen] amid a cloud of dust, we commenced to discharge our revolvers at them, which had the desired effect of stampeding them; they fired but a few shots, and in a few minutes we had full possession of the town; resulting in the capture of six prisoners, nine horses and equipments."

The brigade galloped in minutes later, Grierson leading. The colonel was disturbed to hear that the citizens resisted because they expected the Yankees to hang them and burn the town. Speaking loudly enough to be heard through curtained windows, Grierson swore his men "were not there to interfere with private citizens or to destroy their property or to insult or molest their families, that we were after the soldiers and property of the rebel government."

Because Philadelphia had no military value, the brigade moved south promptly. Grierson took one precaution before leaving. He ordered Colonel Prince and his rear guard to assemble the town's citizens for an unusual ceremony. Surby noted: "The last I saw of them they were standing in line with arms extended perpendicular, and Colonel Prince was swearing them not to give any information for a certain length of time."

On the road from Philadelphia to Decatur, Grierson got unexpected information about the progress of Company B. The two scouts sent the previous night to cut telegraph lines returned after seventy-five miles of continuous riding. Dressed in "Secesh" clothing, they had breezed to within a mile of Macon before being stopped by a Confederate picket. The picket confided that two cavalry regiments and one infantry regiment were positioned in Macon to battle the Yankee raiders. Unable to go forward, the scouts raced back to Louisville and followed the main column's trail south.

Grierson must have experienced mixed emotions about that news. Forbes's Company B had decoyed a powerful force away from the brigade; it may have been too big a force for thirty-six riders to elude.

But Captain Forbes had no desire to retreat before leaving

a mark the enemy would notice. Backing away from Macon, Company B captured a lone Confederate soldier, an unenthusiastic conscript, or draftee. The Confederate was willing to guide Company B to an important railroad bridge below Macon. The party looped back but was disappointed to find the bridge too well guarded to attack. Captain Forbes had no options left: "We were now entitled to overtake the brigade, if we could, and stretched our march for Philadelphia which we knew they must pass on their way to Newton Station." After resting and feeding the horses at a nearby plantation, Company B embarked on a march through the night to intersect the main column at dawn.

The main column was resting on a plantation south of Philadelphia at the same time, but the camp was filled with anticipation. The troopers all knew their objective was the Vicksburg & Jackson Railroad at Newton Station, now a scant twenty-five miles away. Grierson ordered a night march. He commanded Colonel William Blackburn of the Seventh to advance with a battalion of two hundred men given the job of taking the objective. The rest of the brigade would follow an hour behind.

Blackburn spoke to his battalion for more than an hour. Each company was given specific responsibilities on the mission. Blackburn was just as thorough with the scouts. Colonel Grierson left nothing to chance.

Surby's scouts took the point at 10 p.m. Surby had a pleasant ride: "The night was a beautiful starlight one, the roads in good condition, and meeting with no enemy, nothing occurred to interrupt the stillness that reigned until midnight." After midnight, shots rang out that nearly killed him.

Operating in groups of two, the scouts could barely see

ahead of their horses' heads in the darkness. Uncertain of direction at a forking of the road, Surby sent his partner to a nearby farmhouse for information. On his return, Surby's fellow scout mistook Surby for the enemy and rode away firing. That prompted more fire at Surby by other scouts far away in the darkness, too far away to know whom or what they were shooting at. Nerves were raw; the men tasted danger in their throats.

It took half an hour before the misunderstanding was straightened out. Summing up the mishap, Surby said, "Loss sustained, one hat."

By 3 a.m., Surby had begun knocking on doors in the town of Decatur. Colonel Blackburn wanted to know about enemy troop disposition in Newton Station. When Surby finally gained admittance to an inn, the owner obligingly told him there was a military hospital in Newton Station and possibly some infantrymen guarding the station. He did not know how many.

Passing the word back, the scouts moved through Decatur gingerly. Blackburn's battalion followed, then the rest of the brigade.

Far north of Decatur, Hatch was retreating slowly enough to keep Barteau in pursuit. The Iowans were maintaining their distance, though, by burning every bridge they crossed. Hatch confidently swelled the size of his march with booty. Sergeant Pierce recorded that "we soon accumulated about 600 head of horses and mules with about 200 able bodied negroes to lead them."

Of course, the Iowans were not capturing those African-Americans, who were runaway slaves, eagerly seeking freedom behind Union lines. Slaves knew about the Emancipation

Proclamation issued in 1863, knew they could be free in the North. Unfortunately, Grierson could not let runaways attach themselves to the main column and slow down the march. But Hatch was dictating the pace of his march, not the enemy. Even so, Sergeant Pierce regretted that many had to be left behind: "As the colored women and children could not be taken along, they expressed their feeling towards us by running out to the road, as we passed, with a bowl of milk or a pone of corn bread and slice of meat."

As Grierson's force neared Newton Station that night and Hatch's rested outside Tupelo, Barteau's commander, General Ruggles, was stubbornly denying the truth. Unable to accept the fact that the Federals had ridden through his district untouched, he wired Pemberton that the enemy was "falling back before our cavalry." He estimated that Barteau was driving two thousand invaders back northward.

General Pemberton was unconvinced. Going above his superior, he wired directly to President Jefferson Davis for help that night: "I have so little cavalry in this department that I am compelled to divert a portion of my infantry to meet raids in Northern Mississippi. If any troops can possibly be spared . . . I think they should be sent here." Pemberton still thought the danger was far off in northern Mississippi; actually, it was nearly on his doorstep.

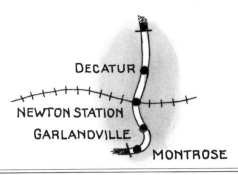

DECATUR

NEWTON STATION
GARLANDVILLE
MONTROSE

DAY EIGHT: FRIDAY, APRIL 24

★ Blackburn's battalion bivouacked six miles north of Newton Station, waiting for the sunrise. Then, Surby wrote, "Colonel Blackburn ordered me to proceed lively with my two men to the station, reconnoiter, and report what force was stationed there, what time the train would arrive, and so forth." Seven days of anticipation and hard travel would end soon in action. The raiders were three hundred miles deep into enemy territory, less than fifty miles east of Pemberton's headquarters in Jackson. They were going to strike the Vicksburg & Jackson Railroad—Vicksburg's supply lifeline.

Galloping "through a timbered country somewhat rolling, and displaying but little cultivation," they reached the outskirts of Newton Station an hour later. Seeing no Confederate pickets in the town, Surby gathered more information from a homeowner at the town's edge. Learning that two trains were expected soon, he dispatched one scout back to Blackburn and sauntered into the town.

A locomotive's whistle in the distance told Surby that there was no time to lose. Finding the telegraph office closed, the

Lieutenant Colonel William D. Blackburn, a battalion commander in the Seventh Illinois. Blackburn led the attack on Newton Station. U.S. ARMY MILITARY HISTORY INSTITUTE

scouts secured the military hospital there. Leveling a revolver at convalescent Confederate soldiers standing in the doorway, Surby barked orders: "Remain inside! Don't come out on peril of your lives!" Just then, Blackburn's battalion charged into town and went into action. Pickets blocked all roads out of town. The rest of the troopers dismounted and positioned themselves in hiding. All were ready as the overtaxed loco-motive chugged into the station pulling twenty-five loaded freight cars. Standing by the station door, Blackburn and his scouts watched the train pull off the main track and come to rest on a sidetrack. On Blackburn's prearranged signal, Federal cavalry troopers swarmed the train and took it.

Only moments passed before a second train approached the station; it was a combined passenger-and-freight train. Surby was ready to pounce: "On she came rounding the curve, her passengers unconscious of the surprise that awaited them. The engineer decreased her speed. She was now nearly opposite the depot. Springing upon the steps of the locomotive, and presenting my revolver at the engineer, I told him if he reversed that engine I would put a ball through him. He was at my mercy, and obeyed orders. It would have done anyone good to have seen the men rush from their hiding places amid the shouts and cheers which rent the air of 'the train is ours.' "

The raiders' combined haul was enormously valuable. The freight train was loaded with ammunition and other military supplies for the armies at Jackson and Vicksburg. It also pulled car after car of railroad ties, bridge timbers, and plank wood. The mixed passenger–freight train was also a prize—four cars were filled with guns and ammunition, six with commissary supplies.

The troopers were jubilant, but Blackburn cut the celebration short. There was work to be done as quickly as possible. A car-by-car inspection and inventory were launched. Freight cars loaded with artillery shells and explosives were quickly moved down the track and away from buildings. An anxious passenger told Colonel Blackburn that two of the freight cars carried his furniture and household goods. Blackburn assigned a squad of men to unload the man's possessions and deposit them in the street. The passenger would have to get them to Vicksburg another way; both trains would be burned.

Shortly, artillery shells began exploding from the fire's heat.

Hearing distant explosions, Grierson feared the worst: Blackburn had been ambushed. Spurring the brigade to a gallop, Grierson arrived in town minutes later to witness triumph, not disaster. The colonel must have been very relieved. The raid had succeeded against nearly impossible odds. He relaxed enough, momentarily, to break his inflexible rule against liquor for men on duty. Seeing troopers filling canteens with whiskey from a confiscated barrel, Grierson turned a blind eye. His troopers deserved a reward.

But there was much more work to do. Two battalions were quickly dispatched along the railroad line, one east, the other west. They were directed to set fire to all bridges and trestlework (supporting frames) they could find and to tear down telegraph poles and cut the wire into foot-long pieces.

Troopers remaining in Newton Station searched its buildings for military supplies and tools. They burned a warehouse holding over five hundred handguns and piles of new Confederate uniforms. They used tools to pry up the long iron railroad tracks of the main line. After heating the rails on one of several bonfires, teams of men strained to twist and deform those massive iron bars.

In the midst of raging fires and clanging metal and men yelling and laughing, two of Grierson's officers sat calmly at a table copying out lengthy legal documents. They were writing "paroles" for the seventy-five captured Confederate hospital patients.

During the Civil War, some prisoners of war were actually imprisoned, but many were paroled. They were released

Union soldiers and two civilians proudly pose with this recently wrecked locomotive. LIBRARY OF CONGRESS

in their own custody with a handwritten paper saying when and where they had been captured. Prisoners were then honor-bound not to fight again until they were officially exchanged for prisoners from the opposing side. By paroling the seventy-five hospital patients in Newton Station, Grierson was reducing the enemy's army by seventy-five men without firing a shot. The parole system later broke down because the Confederacy refused to exchange African-American soldiers. The Confederacy said African-Americans fighting for the Union were stolen property, not legitimate soldiers. The U.S. government rejected that position and suspended prisoner exchange. The program was on-again, off-again for nearly

a year until General Grant permanently stopped exchanges in 1864.

By mid-afternoon Grierson had become satisfied with the work done in Newton Station. The raiders had struck a painful blow in the heart of the enemy's territory; the mission was gloriously successful thus far. The harder part lay ahead—getting home.

"From captured mails and information obtained by my scouts I knew that large forces had been sent out to intercept our return," Grierson wrote in his *Record of Services*. Retracing their steps to La Grange was out of the question. Ordered to lead his brigade back to safety "as I might thereafter deem best," Grierson directed his officers to ask paroled Confederates about the alternative routes eastward. The brigade then marched south, competing for the road with a makeshift caravan of local citizens. With Newton Station in flames, people for miles around panicked and fled the area with whatever food and personal belongings they could carry.

Five miles below Newton Station, Grierson ordered a short bivouac. "The forced marches which I was compelled to make, in order to reach this point successfully, necessarily very much fatigued and exhausted my command, and rest and food were absolutely necessary for its safety . . . After resting about three hours we moved south towards Garlandville," Grierson said.

Garlandville was ready for them. "At this point we found the citizens, many of them venerable with age, armed with shotguns and organized to resist our approach." A cavalry charge failed to disperse them, and one trooper was wounded before the raiders took the town. Grierson gave the townspeople a fatherly lecture: "After disarming them, we showed them the folly of their actions, and released them. Without an exception they acknowledged their mistake, and declared that they had been grossly deceived as to our real character."

With the effort to put more distance between his brigade and Newton Station, Sergeant Surby wrote, "we started again, feeling somewhat old and tired." The column slowly ambled southwest into dark forests of pine that turned into swampy bottoms. Lulled by exhaustion and the monotonous motion, the riders were led by their horses. "The men were so sleepy and tired that nothing but a shot fired would arouse them," said Surby.

At one point, Surby awoke to find his mount contentedly nibbling a clump of grass. Unable to locate his fellow scouts in the night's blackness, Surby crawled about on hands and knees until he could feel the road. "To get on the right course was the next thing; this I did by feeling for the toe and heel of the horse-shoe prints," he wrote. "After traveling about two miles I was rewarded by overtaking the rear-guard to the column. I assure you I felt relieved."

He felt relieved too soon. Once again ahead of the column, Surby had a life-threatening misadventure. The scout happened upon a corral with several desirable horses. While trying to catch a new mount, an officer from the Sixth Illinois rode up to the same corral, saw the shotgun and civilian saddle on Surby's horse, and assumed that he had caught a Confederate. In the darkness, Surby sneaked around his fellow Federal and got the drop on him. Unfortunately, another Sixth Illinois trooper had come on the scene before Surby, and the officers got close enough to see each other. The third trooper fired and instantly regretted it. He recognized the "Confederate" yelling

Bending iron railroad tracks like this required a blazing fire to heat the metal and a number of strong hands to do the bending. LIBRARY OF CONGRESS

in pain as Surby. Luckily, the ball had grazed the soft flesh inches above Surby's hipbone. When the incident was shared among all the troopers, Surby wrote, "They allowed it was a good joke, but I could not view it in that light . . . For a few days it burned and smarted considerable."

After midnight, they found a plantation and halted for the night. "For the first time in forty hours did we take off our saddles from our weary horses," Surby remembered.

Grierson and his officers probably congratulated each other

that night. They probably thought about the plight of their detached forces, the decoys, too. The Quinine Brigade, the less effectives, was already back in La Grange, Tennessee. They returned without any losses. Hatch's Iowans and Company B were less fortunate.

Hatch, thinking he was well ahead of Barteau, detoured to strike the Mobile & Ohio Railroad again. The determined Tennessee Confederate caught up with the Iowans' rear guard while the raiders were torching Newton Station. Forming a defensive line, the Iowans held off three charges with the superior firepower of their repeating rifles. A fourth charge broke their line, and the rear guard joined the rest of the regiment. Hatch commanded a second defensive stand that stopped Barteau's forces again. As Barteau tried to wheel his cavalry around the Iowans' flank, Hatch had his command fall back across a bridge and burn it.

Barteau's pursuit of Hatch was over. There was no point in fording the river and continuing the chase; Barteau's troops were completely out of ammunition. While Barteau supervised the burial of the dozens of men he had lost, word of the raid on Newton Station arrived by rider.

The Iowans survived several firefights without a loss that day, but the Illinoisans of Company B did not. They approached Philadelphia about noon. Three troopers disguised as Confederates met three real Confederates at the door of a house outside the town. The real rebels called the Federals spies and began firing. Hearing shots, the rest of Company B charged ahead. "We galloped down the road," said Sergeant Forbes, "and within about half a mile . . . we saw one of our men, dead on his back in the middle of the road." Another was wounded.

"We left our dead soldier stretched on a Southern porch," reported his brother, Captain Forbes, "under solemn promise from the householder that he would decently bury him." Anxious to rejoin the brigade, they were slowed again by a company of home guards in Philadelphia itself. After a casualty-free skirmish, Company B captured thirty of the local soldiers, wrote paroles, destroyed their weapons, and took some of their fresh horses in trade.

Captain Forbes decided to push on without rest, following the main column's trail. Sergeant Stephen Forbes remembered their uneasiness: "The guerilla and the bushwhacker and the ambush by the roadside, familiar to us from two years' service in the field, were in all our minds as we rode that day through the thickety woods, scanning every cover and watchful of every turn in the road."

At day's end, General Pemberton seemed more unnerved than any of the Federals. He was astonished by what Grierson had accomplished. He was worried about what might happen next. He feared the raiders might turn west from Newton Station and attack Jackson—his headquarters and the state capital. But wherever the Federals went, Pemberton was determined that they should not escape.

The Confederate sent two infantry regiments and an artillery battery to form a defensive line halfway between Jackson and Newton Station. He ordered General Chalmers to block a northeast escape route: "Move with all your cavalry and light artillery via Oxford to Okolona to intercept force of enemy now at Newton." He also ordered other troops to block a northeastern route. And just in case they tried going south toward Baton Rouge, Pemberton wired this order to General

Franklin Gardner at Port Hudson: "Send all your disposable cavalry in direction of Tangipahoa, to intercept."

Pemberton did not act on the other news that day: General Grant now had more than thirty thousand soldiers on the Louisiana side of the river and appeared poised to cross over and attack Mississippi.

RALEIGH   MONTROSE

DAY NINE: SATURDAY, APRIL 25

★ "Tall, with dark complexion, hazel eyes, black hair and beard, and prominent nose. Though not robust in appearance, he has an iron constitution, and is capable of enduring great hardships and fatigue; modest and unassuming in his manner." That is how Sergeant Surby proudly described his commander, Colonel Benjamin H. Grierson. As a member of the Seventh Illinois, Surby had never served with Grierson previously. But he had seen enough during the raid to form a very strong impression: "Colonel Grierson was not one of the retreating kind; his motto was 'onward.'"

So, after a well-deserved night's rest and a leisurely breakfast of roast pork and coffee, the brigade switched directions again. Rather than retreating to the north, east, or south, Grierson ordered the column west—into the teeth of the enemy. They rode parallel to the Vicksburg Railroad toward Grand Gulf.

Grierson knew from previous conversations with General Grant "that the objective point was Vicksburg and that all his operations would lead to getting a foothold on firm ground, and then to fight it out for a final capture of that stronghold. From my study of maps and knowledge gained otherwise of the country, I needed nothing more to convince me as to the approximate route Grant's forces would eventually take." Grant needed the Illinois cavalry, Grierson reasoned, to assault Vicksburg. The colonel ordered a slow march that morning to rest both men and horses. He sent a number of search parties to scour the woods for fresh horses; many troopers were riding mules because lamed horses had been left behind. Prospects were poor, though. The brigade had left the rich cotton-plantation area and plunged into the Piney Woods region of Mississippi.

The Butternut Guerrillas found badly rutted roads, bridge-less streams, and few farms in the Piney Woods. For the most part, the up-country white farmers in this part of the state scratched out a living without the help of slaves. If his fellow Northerners rode along with him, Sergeant Surby thought, they "would be bitterly disappointed . . . they would find a double log cabin or frame house, with plain furniture (very scant), a feint show of comfort . . . fields that show a lack of proper cultivation. Altogether, there is no show of wealth . . . No free schools to educate their children, and not sufficient wealth to send them from home." The country was also a hotbed of resistance to the Confederate government's con-scription, or draft, of men for the army. The woods were filled with men in hiding, army deserters and draft dodgers ready to bushwhack Confederate government agents or Federal sol-diers.

By midday, Surby and his fellow scouts had located a planta-tion owned by a Mr. Nichol, and the column stopped for a meal. The brigade had begun eating entirely off the land by this time; even the hardtack had run out.

Searching for horse fodder, the troopers encountered the

darkest side of slavery. Surby observed, "While here some of the men found a negro imprisoned in a log-hut, with manacles fastened about both ankles, and a chain attached to it, fastened to a ring in the floor . . . it was a sickening sight to look at those ankles; the flesh was worn off to the bone and almost in a state of mortification . . . His only offense for all this treatment was trying to run away from bondage." After receiving medical treatment, the slave was offered a mount and a place in the brigade. He accepted both gladly, as so many other runaway slaves did. Before the war's end, more than 179,000 African-Americans volunteered and served in the Federal army; another 20,000 were sailors.

By no means were all Federal soldiers in favor of African-American emancipation. In 1861, the majority probably opposed it. They were fighting for the reunion of the states under the Constitution, which had protected the rights of slaveholders. Opinions were divided even in the Grierson household. Ben Grierson's wife, Alice, was a lifelong abolitionist. She risked being jailed before the war by secretly teaching reading and writing to runaway slaves on their Underground Railway journey to Canada. She was convinced that the war was God's punishment of the American people because "they will not let the slaves go free." Grierson, like his idol Abraham Lincoln, was uncertain about the future of slavery when the conflict began.

But as the war progressed and Northerners witnessed the reality of slavery firsthand, opinion shifted. The bravery of African-American combatants contributed to new perspectives. One Union officer had this to say about a black regiment under the command of Henry Ward Beecher, brother of the author of *Uncle Tom's Cabin*: "I never [would] have believed

Farriers, men who shod horses, kept the mounts healthy in camps. Anvils, hammers, shoes, and nails could not be carried on field operations, so troopers had to "trade" with civilians for healthy mounts. LIBRARY OF CONGRESS

that a common plantation negro could be brought to face a white man. I supposed that everything in the shape of spirit & self respect had been crushed out of them generations back, but am glad to find myself mistaken . . . There is a firmness & determination in their looks & in the way in which they handle a musket that I like." After a major battle, an Illinois infantryman wrote his mother: "When you hear eney one say that negro soldiers wont fight just tell them that they ly." Suffering more casualties—from battle wounds and disease—than whites, African-American soldiers earned the respect of their comrades and superiors alike.

The brigade took an unusually large amount of meat, corn,

and mules from the Nichol plantation, possibly to teach its owner a lesson. Traveling uneventfully until dark, the troopers stopped at another plantation for the night. Before retiring, Grierson chose one Butternut Guerrilla scout, Samuel Nelson, to perform a little night mischief. He dispatched the scout north to Forest Station, where he would destroy telegraph wires.

Nelson never completed his mission, another piece of good fortune for the raiders. He ran into Confederate cavalry riding to intercept the Federals. That morning, Captain Robert C. Love, stationed east of Jackson, received this urgent telegram from General John Pemberton: "Ascertain where the enemy is and go in that direction . . . and get on his rear, and plant an ambush and annoy him. See if something can be done." Surprised to receive a direct order from the commanding general, Love rounded up all the troops available and sped toward Raleigh.

Love's command happened upon the lone scout near midnight. Pretending to be a citizen forced to help the Yankees, Nelson estimated the brigade's strength at eighteen hundred men and told Love they were moving east to attack the Mobile & Ohio Railroad. After watching the Confederates march out, Nelson doubled back to the brigade's night camp. Love was certain to discover the deception from horse tracks in the road, and the brigade had to be warned.

Ironically, it was Captain Henry Forbes's bad fortune that day to be taken in by Grierson's deceptions. When the members of Company B rode into the smoldering ruins of Newton Station that morning, they sought information from patients at the Confederate military hospital. Grierson had left the mistaken impression in Newton Station that the brigade was

moving east. That notion corroborated Colonel Prince's sug-
gestion that the brigade would retire east to Alabama. Forbes
knew that Grierson went south leaving Newton Station and
assumed that action to be a feint. He decided that the brigade
had gone south before swinging back to the east. With a hard
ride due east, Forbes reasoned, Company B could catch the
brigade when it reached the town of Enterprise, the next logi-
cal target of the raid.

The troopers departed immediately, riding in the wrong direction. Captain Forbes said, "All rumors agreed that there
were no Rebels in Enterprise," but in the town they discovered
a guarded stockade. The captain and four troopers approached
it. "Halting a moment, we borrowed a pocket handkerchief
from a wash hanging in one of the door-yards, fastened it to
the end of a saber, and under this as a flag of truce rode down
to demand a conference." The Confederate pickets passed
word inside, and three officers emerged momentarily, also
waving a white cloth.

One Confederate officer asked, "To what are we indebted
for the honor of this visit?"

"I come from Major General Grierson. To demand the surrender of Enterprise," Captain Forbes asserted.

Calmly the Confederate officer asked, "Will you put the demand in writing?" When Captain Forbes was told to address
his surrender demand to a colonel, he knew that a regiment or
better was stationed in Enterprise. Continuing his bluff, he
gave the Confederates one hour to comply, "after which further delay will be at your peril." Both sides retreated to await
surrender or, more likely, battle. That's probably what the
Confederates thought; Captain Forbes had a better idea:

*We never officially knew what the Confederates' reply was, as
for reasons best known to themselves they failed to make it
reach us. Perhaps it was lack of speed. We fell back, very
cheerfully, four miles, and fed, and resumed our retreat, which
was diligently continued all night. We learned afterwards from
the Southern papers that our reply was forwarded six miles on
our track that evening with an escort of 2,000 infantry, under
the impression that we were at least 1,500 strong.*

*Once more we were out of the lion's mouth, but woefully and
inextricably entangled in his den. We rode on towards the
sinking sun and—planned. Should we run north? Should we
attempt Pensacola, Mobile, Vicksburg? We determined on one
more despairing effort at a stern chase of the regiments. We had
lost another forty miles. The nearest point where we were certain
of the whereabouts of our command was Garlandville.*

They received an unexpected welcome in Garlandville:
"Here was a home guard of sixty men (the Garlandville
Avengers) who had sworn to fight at sight any Yanks they
might encounter. Our scouts fell in with one of these guards
and actually accompanied him to warn his companions that
we were Alabama cavalry, fearing that they might mistake us
for Yankees and give us trouble!" Company B passed through
town at dusk, so covered in dirt that nobody guessed they
were wearing Federal blue uniforms.

After numerous conversations with cooperative slaves, Company B's scouts were certain of the brigade's true direction,
west toward Raleigh. They stayed on that path long past midnight, and then rested for a few hours.

RALEIGH

WESTVILLE

DAY TEN: SUNDAY, APRIL 26

⭐ Before dawn, Samuel Nelson rode up to the brigade's picket line and dashed to wake Colonel Grierson. Recounting his chance encounter with Captain Love, Nelson was unsure how many troopers Love commanded. He just knew that the Confederate was eager to face Grierson's "1,800 Yankees." Love's command may have been the advance party of a much larger force. As Grierson later said about Love's near miss, "They were on the direct road to our camp, and had they not been turned from their course would have come up with us before daylight." Grierson had to sense that the net was tightening, that the trap was about to be sprung on his brigade.

The regimental buglers played "Boots and Saddles," and the troopers were ready to march in minutes. Three men had to be left behind—one was seriously wounded at Garlandville, the other two were too sick to ride. The brigade's overnight host, Dr. Mackadora, was willing to care for them on his plantation, even though the raiders had confiscated and eaten much of his stored supplies.

Grierson had to make a difficult choice that morning. As the column approached a bridge crossing the Leaf River, he knew that burning it would delay his pursuers. It would also delay Company B. Weighing the options, he chose to protect the greater number. The bridge was in flames as the last troopers crossed over.

That action initiated the burning of every bridge the brigade crossed that day. By mid-morning, rain had begun falling; by noon, the rain had become torrential. The already-swollen streams flooded rapidly and would be hazardous to ford. Bridge-burning bought the brigade precious time.

The brigade started its tenth day approximately one hundred miles from Grand Gulf. Grierson forced a rapid pace along the sloppy roads. At Raleigh, the scouts found virtually no activity. One man jumped his horse and galloped away ahead of the incoming scouts. The man was easily captured and proved to be the sheriff. His saddlebags were filled with Confederate money—the county treasury. The sheriff was turned over to the main column for questioning, and the march proceeded.

At nightfall, the brigade marched unopposed through Westville and bivouacked at a plantation beyond town. It had taken so many twists and turns that it might have been "ahead of information" again. The troopers had met no armed resistance all day.

But Grierson was filled with urgency. To reach Grand Gulf, the raiders had to leave the Piney Woods and cross more populous countryside. Then they had to cross the well-guarded tracks of the New Orleans & Jackson Railroad before streaking toward Grant's landing place. As Stephen Forbes said, strategy and speed were the keys to a cavalry raid. Boldness and surprise were essential too.

Two vital river crossings lay ahead; Grierson decided they

had to be taken that night. He ordered the Seventh to advance to the only bridge on the Strong River, three miles forward, and capture it. After that, two battalions, commanded by Colonel Prince, would advance to the Pearl River ferry and secure it. The brigade's survival depended on it: "Though tired and sleepy," Sergeant Surby said, "there were those who did not rest or sleep longer than to feed their horses and prepare supper. As the citizens were arming themselves, and the news was flying in every direction, it was a matter of life or death that Pearl River should be crossed and the New Orleans and Southern railroad reached, without any delay."

The drum corps of the Ninety-third New York Infantry in 1864. Music in the army went far beyond the bugler's reveille and "Boots and Saddles." The Seventh Illinois's roster listed fourteen members of its regimental band. LIBRARY OF CONGRESS

The tenth day was also a life-and-death struggle for Company B. Here is Stephen Forbes's stirring account:

After a rapid breakfast by the light of our camp fires we started for the hardest and most discouraging ride of the raid. Approaching Raleigh, we repeated in substance the exploit at Philadelphia, surprising, by a headlong charge, a company of home guards which had gathered at the village inn . . . We were now but seven or eight hours behind the regiment, and hope began to dawn, when we came to a stream swollen with recent rains. The column had crossed on a bridge [over the Leaf River], which was now a wreck of blackened timbers. Grierson had given us up as lost and was burning his bridges behind him. Five times that day we swam our horses across overflowing streams, and once were compelled to make a long detour to find a place where we could get into the water and out again.

And then a greater danger loomed ahead of us. Some thirty or forty miles farther on was Strong river, and a few miles beyond that the Pearl, neither of which we could hope to ford or swim; and we were losing time, by reason of the burned bridges, instead of gaining on Grierson. Some way must be found to reach him before he destroyed Strong river bridge or we were lost; and so the captain called for volunteers to ride on and overtake the column. Three of us, who answered the call mounted on the best and freshest horses of the company, leaving our arms and all encumbrances behind excepting only a pistol apiece and a few loose cartridges in our pockets, left the company at a gallop at about 5:00 o'clock in the afternoon . . .

A few miles on the way we saw a group of saddled horses in the brush, a little distance from the road, with no riders in

sight. We listened for shots as we hurried by, but they did not
come. A little after sundown the trail we were following simply
stopped in a grassy field and went no farther. Puzzled at first,
we presently suspected a countermarch, and following the trail
back through the thickening dusk about half a mile, we found
where it branched off to the left. If we had been a little later we
should have been completely lost. Black night now fell, with
drizzling rain, and we dismounted now and then to make sure,
by feeling the road, that we were still on the track of the
regiments. And by and by we began to hear through the trees
faint sounds of a marching column a mile or so ahead. Pushing
our tired horses to their best, we presently drew near Grierson's
rear guard. "Halt! Who comes there?" some one called out to us
. . . "Company B." Instantly a great cheer arose, "Company B
has come back," and . . . it ran down the column, cheer upon
cheer, faster than our horses could run. Great was our welcome
when we reached Grierson, just as his horse's hoofs were
rattling on the Strong river bridge, and repeated to him the
vigorous message committed to us: "Captain Forbes presents his
compliments, and begs to be allowed to burn his bridges for
himself."

It must have pleased Grierson enormously to hear Forbes's
clever wordplay. He debriefed the sergeant speedily: What
route had they taken, what enemy had they faced, how far
back was the remainder of Company B? There was no time for
pleasantries, though. Grierson detached a squadron to hold
the bridge until Company B's arrival and sped on toward the
Pearl River ferry. All sources said that it was the only crossing
for twenty-five miles in either direction.

Grierson would have been doubly pleased to know that

Colonel Hatch and the Second Iowa regiment arrived that day in La Grange. After being detached as a decoy unit, the Iowans fought two pitched battles and skirmished continually for five days. The regiment suffered ten casualties in the process: six were taken prisoner at Palo Alto, three were wounded, one was killed by a bushwhacker within a few miles of La Grange. That was a comparatively light price to pay in the Civil War. Casualty rates of 25 percent were common in major battles; the Iowans' rate was less than 2 percent.

And their achievement was great. By diverting Barteau's mixed unit—his Second Tennessee Cavalry and General Ruggles's Mississippi state troops—the Iowans allowed Grierson's brigade to reach Newton Station unscathed. They were unable to sting the Mobile & Ohio Railroad, but did burn tons of baled cotton and destroyed large quantities of military supplies. Additionally, Hatch arrived in camp with fifty-one Confederate prisoners, an uncounted number of runaway slaves, three hundred rifles, and two hundred horses and mules. Hatch estimated enemy casualties were at least one hundred dead and wounded.

General Pemberton, isolated in his Jackson headquarters and flooded with misinformation from his commanders, reported a victory that night: "Enemy, who were at Okolona [Hatch], driven back. Defeated them at Birmingham, killing some 20 and wounding many others." This telegram to General Johnston ended: "These raids cannot be prevented unless I can have more mounted men."

Pemberton's next decision made intercepting the raiders considerably more difficult. General John Adams, commanding at Lake Station on the Vicksburg Railroad, correctly assessed the raiders at about eight hundred men headed west to threaten the railroad. Pemberton ignored that report and believed the telegraph message from Enterprise: the raiders were in eastern Mississippi, demanding the surrender of Enterprise. The Confederate was certain that Grierson would turn north to escape. Pemberton sent this message to General Chalmers in the north: "Move, with all your cavalry and light artillery, via Oxford, to Okolona, to intercept force of enemy."

That was exactly the same message he had sent three days earlier. It would not work better this time. Chalmers was dispatched to pursue a phantom skillfully constructed by the devious mind of Colonel Benjamin Grierson. Pemberton was certain that Grierson's brigade was two hundred miles east of Jackson that night and riding north; the troopers were actually less than thirty miles from his headquarters, streaking west.

HAZLEHURST

DAY ELEVEN: MONDAY, APRIL 27

⭐ Day ten passed into day eleven, unmarked by coffee boiled over a campfire or sleep on a damp spot of earth. The brigade was in continuous motion, stretched out across miles of unlit countryside.

Colonel Prince led two battalions toward the Pearl River ferry. The remainder of the Seventh Illinois followed, then Grierson riding with the Sixth Illinois. At the rear, Sergeant Forbes and a squadron of troopers guarded the Strong River bridge and awaited the arrival of Company B.

Hours before dawn, the scouts reported to Colonel Prince. They saw no Confederate guards on their side of the Pearl River; the boat was docked on the opposite shore. Prince and the scouts rode down to the river, his battalions left behind. There was no light in the ferryman's house and no activity on the shore. Prince ordered a scout to swim the river on horseback. The scout was nearly dragged under by the swift-moving river and struggled back to the shore. Uncertain what his next move would be, Prince saw the ferryman, shrugging off sleep, walk to the shore. "You-all want across?" the ferryman asked.

Prince, adopting a Southern drawl, claimed to be with the

First Alabama Cavalry and asked for passage. Minutes later, a slave poled the flat-bottomed boat across the river and docked. Twenty-four men and their horses crammed aboard and slowly crossed the river, Prince anxiously awaiting the result.

There were no guards on the other side. The boat returned to begin the tedious crossing and recrossing of the river. Forty round-trips were necessary to get the brigade over the river.

As the second group was poled across, rear-guard pickets rode in with a prisoner. He was a Confederate courier, minutes late, riding to warn the ferryman that Yankees were coming. Grierson's urgency had paid off.

Arriving at sunup, Grierson ordered Prince and his two battalions forward to the New Orleans & Jackson Railroad. Grierson remained to supervise the crossing of the brigade. At this juncture, they were far ahead of information again and well disguised by dirt. "Our troops were taken for the First Alabama Cavalry from Mobile," Grierson wrote. "I receipted the ferryman for the passage . . . [and] accepted an invitation to breakfast with my officers at a fine home near the ferry. The breakfast was well served, the ladies were all smiles, when up came some blunderhead and blurted out something to me about the 'Sixth Illinois Cavalry,' and what they were doing. The countenances of the hosts changed and some persons immediately left the room."

During the meal, Grierson concocted a scheme certain to confuse and unnerve his enemy Pemberton. He penciled this message as the commanding officer of the First Alabama: "The Yankees have advanced to Pearl River, but finding the ferry destroyed they could not cross, and have left, taking a northeasterly direction." A scout was dispatched with the message and ordered to send it to Pemberton, via telegraph, after Colonel Prince secured a station on the New Orleans & Jackson Railroad.

While the Pearl River crossing continued hour after hour, Sergeant Forbes still waited for Company B at the Strong River bridge. They were very late. They were lost.

Shortly after Sergeant Forbes and his two fellow volunteers galloped to catch the brigade, Captain Forbes and Company B took on a guide. He was a farmer who offered a shortcut through the woods to the main road. Hours later, "twisting and turning, this way and that, through the tangle of fallen tree trunks, they [Company B] lost, not only their way, but all sense of direction likewise," the captain wrote later. The members of Company B bivouacked eventually and waited for dawn. Finding their way to the road, they recognized the main column's tracks and followed. At the Strong River, they celebrated by burning the bridge with the guard detachment; all then raced ahead to the Pearl River. Company B and its escort arrived at the ferry at two that afternoon, just as the last boatload of troopers was about to cross. It was incredible timing. Arriving half an hour later, they would have been hopelessly stranded after the ferry was set ablaze.

Colonel Grierson said much honor was due the men of Company B for the courage and skill they showed. In an unpublished manuscript, Captain Forbes summarized the mission proudly and with emotion: "We were now once more with friends on the west side of the Pearl. We had been absent five days and four nights; we had marched fully three hundred miles in ten different counties, had captured and paroled forty prisoners, confronted and evaded several thousand of the Confederate troops at Macon and Enterprise; slipped through the home guards of six county towns, been twice misled and once lost; had had but eighteen hours of sleep, while rations for man and horse had been for the most part conspicuous by their absence. We simply had not had time to eat. The men who did this work *were a year and a half from the plow-tail,* and their chief claim to consideration is that they were representative men—fair types of our American citizen-soldiery."

As the tedious river crossings continued, Prince and his battalions were advancing fourteen miles to Hazlehurst, a junction on the north-to-south-running New Orleans & Jackson Railroad. Sergeant Surby and the Butternut Guerrillas scouted the way.

The countryside changed again before them. The Piney Woods gave way to rocky outcrops and rolling land dotted with small fields of cotton and corn. News of the Federals' approach preceded them; families were in flight along the road. Surby stopped to speak with an unlikely defender: "One small man, with sandy whiskers and foxy eyes, trying to look as savage as a meat-axe, had secured in an old belt around his waist two large old flint-lock dragoon pistols . . . and an old United States musket, flint-lock. As I came up to him he brought his gun to a carry arms, and between a grin and a laugh exclaimed: 'They is coming, Capting, and I am ready; I just bid the old lady good-bye, and told her she need not expect me back until I had killed four Yankees and they were exterminated from our Southern *sile* [soil].' " Nearer town, the scouts encountered a dozen armed men lazily awaiting the Yankees' arrival. After surreptitiously surrounding them, the scouts confiscated and destroyed their weapons. Colonel Prince arrived soon after and gave Surby the bogus telegram Colonel Grierson had written to General Pemberton. When the scouts reached the sleepy little town, Surby and four scouts hung back while two scouts delivered the telegram.

The telegraph office, like most, was housed in the train station. Inside, the scouts walked past six Confederate soldiers waiting for a train and gave the telegraph operator Grierson's message. The operator grilled the scouts: What unit were they from? Who was their commander? The scouts must have sounded calm and natural; the telegraph operator tapped out the message, the Confederate soldiers ignored them, and, mission accomplished, the scouts left the building.

While the scouts were walking back to their mounts, a horseman charged them and yelled, "Help! Help! Stop the Yankees!" It was the sheriff the scouts had captured the previous day. During the long night march, he had freed himself, stolen a horse, and escaped. Now he was leveling a revolver at the scouts as he alerted the town.

The sheriff did not fire, so the scouts ran around the building. As the scouts mounted, they saw Confederate soldiers in pursuit, making the scouts fire over the Confederates' heads. Surby wasted no time thinking. He sent one scout up the nearest telegraph pole to cut the town's communications; a second scout raced back to tell Prince. In short order, two battalions galloped onto the main street with sabers and revolvers drawn. They secured the now-empty town—the Confederates, the telegraph operator, and the sheriff had all fled—and looked for desperately needed food.

Discovering eggs, ham, and flour stored in the station depot, the troopers carried it across the street to be cooked in a hotel kitchen. As the men relished a hot meal, they lost track of time and were not prepared as a train neared town. The troopers dashed to horse, but the train's engineer saw them coming, coolly stopped his locomotive, reversed it, and escaped by backing up the track.

They had lost a valuable prize and let the enemy escape. That momentary lapse of discipline by Colonel Prince's command could be very costly. In a matter of minutes, the escaped railroad engineer would send Pemberton the raiders' current position. But Prince expected to be long gone before Pemberton could react to that information.

Details searched for military supplies and found a bonanza. Five hundred loaded artillery shells, cases of rifle ammunition, and tons of commissary and quartermaster supplies were in warehouses attached to the station. Prince had it all loaded onto freight cars before burning—the railroad buildings stood too close for safety to private buildings. Bad luck overtook good planning; flaming material was blown onto rooftops by a sudden windstorm. Two buildings caught fire and citizens rushed from their homes to quench the flames before they spread any farther. The winds had brought drenching rains, but the fires were growing anyway.

The Illinois troopers sprang into action. For nearly an hour the people of Hazlehurst and the Yankee soldiers worked together, dousing the flames with buckets of water. Hearing shots in the distance—ammunition exploding in the fire—Grierson ordered the Sixth to charge. Reaching town, he found dozens of troopers camouflaged even further by wet soot and ash. The amateur firefighters from Illinois had extinguished all the fires before any serious damage was done to civilian property. The cavalrymen and the townspeople congratulated each other on a job well done.

Long before the fires in Hazlehurst were quenched, General Pemberton read the railroad engineer's report. Grierson was thirty-five miles southwest of his office. Pemberton had thousands of soldiers searching for him a hundred miles east or north. Pemberton decided that Grierson's intent must be to strike somewhere against Vicksburg's defenses.

He ordered artillery at Vicksburg moved out to protect a vital bridge over the Big Black River which Grierson might target. He ordered infantry regiments to deploy themselves along other bridges and trestlework. Days earlier, Pemberton had ordered General Gardner's cavalry at Port Hudson to guard against Grierson's escape to the south. Now he ordered it north to intercept Grierson. Orders went out to Lieutenant Colonel Barteau in the northeastern part of the state: "Send a courier to Barteau to continue on down as rapidly as possible to Hazlehurst." Pemberton stripped Grand Gulf of its cavalry defense. He ordered Colonel William Wirt Adams to follow the raiders "without delay. Annoy and ambush them if possible. Move rapidly."

But as Pemberton's sense of urgency escalated, Grierson's seemed to subside. Rather than leaving Hazlehurst hurriedly, he assigned detachments to rip up railroad track and cut telegraph lines north and south of town. By day's end, considerable damage had been accomplished, and all the men and horses had a hearty meal. At seven that evening the brigade rode west.

The brigade was now roughly fifty miles from Grand Gulf. Grierson had to wonder whether Grant would be there to meet him. None of the local people he interrogated had heard about large troop movements on the Mississippi; he heard no artillery shelling in the distance. If Grant's plans had changed, riding to Grand Gulf would be disastrous. As Sergeant Surby summarized, whatever course they took was perilous: "It now became necessary to use every precaution. We had passed within twenty-five miles of the capital of the State . . . couriers were flying in every direction, spreading the news, forces were concentrating and sent to intercept us, hem us in and annihilate us . . . They certainly had every advantage on their side;—a perfect knowledge of the country— . . . forces above us and below us on the railroad, in our front at Port Gibson, Grand Gulf and Port Hudson—following our rear—retreat was impossible, even if such an idea had occurred to us, we having destroyed our only hope in that quarter—bridges and ferries."

In fact, General Grant's plans had not changed; his assault had been delayed. That night he wired Washington: "I am now embarking troops for the attack on Grand Gulf. Expect to reduce it tomorrow."

Grierson initiated a new diversion in the hamlet of Gallatin, where six roads crossed. Rather than continuing on the road to Grand Gulf, the brigade followed the road to Natchez instead. He counted on that news reaching Pemberton's headquarters before dawn.

To his men, Grierson's instincts must have seemed miraculous. Minutes after it had changed direction, an unexpected prize fell into the brigade's lap: a sixty-four-pounder heavy-artillery piece, a wagonload of ammunition, and fourteen hundred pounds of gunpowder traveling to Grand Gulf. After destroying the shipment and paroling the Confederates hauling it, Grierson called a halt at a plantation near Hargraves. The colonel, and most of his nearly 950 men, slept for the first time in more than two days.

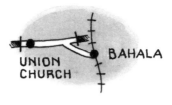

UNION CHURCH   BAHALA

DAY TWELVE: TUESDAY, APRIL 28

★ The brigade began marching along the road toward Natchez at six and halted four hours later. Grierson convened a war council with his senior officers. At some point he aimed to turn north and ride off-road to join Grant at Grand Gulf, but not just yet. The colonel had shared his major concerns earlier with his staff. He had prior knowledge that Grant would cross the Mississippi on April 25. Three days later, that still hadn't happened.

Grierson's second concern was lack of enemy resistance: Why hadn't they been attacked yet? Was the Confederacy much weaker than they thought? Or was a devastating blow being planned somewhere ahead? Nobody had answers. Grierson's only option was to continue to play the game better than his opponents. He recognized that "the greatest generalship, the utmost care and vigilance was necessary for the safety of my command." Grierson was up to the challenge: "The enemy had every advantage . . . they had forces above and below on the railroad, in front from Port Hudson to Vicksburg on the river, and in rear everywhere in all direction. What should hinder them from annihilating myself and small command: One

thing only was in the way and that was there were two parties
to that little transaction . . . I considered what Generals Gardner and Pemberton and other rebel commanders would do as
capable military men and what they would expect me to do
and then I did not do . . . what was expected of me."

He decided that another noisy, destructive attack against the
New Orleans & Jackson Railroad would divide the enemy's attention. He sent four companies under Captain George Trafton
southeast to the junction at Bahala (now named Beauregard,
Mississippi). The invaluable Sergeant Surby was sent as scout.

The brigade proceeded slowly toward the town of Union
Church. At 2 p.m., the troopers stopped at a plantation two
miles west of town to feed their mounts. Grierson gave orders

to maintain a battle-ready status after the horses were unsaddled and fed, but before that was possible "our pickets were fired upon by a considerable force," Grierson reported later.

Every trooper in the brigade had seen combat before; every one had fought bravely. But a surprise cavalry attack, the unexpected shock of galloping horses and gunfire, disorients everyone. Panic can easily take over, but it did not. Stephen Forbes wrote this description of a sneak attack in his journal in 1864: "In a short time the camp was all in confusion, men run-

One wrong move by Colonel Grierson could have landed most of his command in a Confederate prison for the duration of the war. Many could have been held in this windowless structure over the Pearl River near Jackson, Mississippi.
HARPER'S WEEKLY

ning as fast as they could in every direction, carrying saddles, leading horses on the gallop, gathering up carbines and sabers and buckling on belts, while the air was filled with cries and oaths and quick impulsive exclamations and sharp stern orders and shouts of 'Get out of my way there!' 'Catch my horse!' 'Who's got my gun!' 'Fall in here, men quick! Dry up that noise and load your guns!' 'Gallop—March!' "

Discipline and training helped turn the tide. Squadrons fell into line on foot and threw a concentrated line of fire into the charging Confederate cavalry. The rebels abandoned their attack and retreated toward Union Church. Grierson ordered a battalion of the Sixth to pursue. The Confederates rode through and past the small town dominated by a church on a hill. The men of the Sixth dismounted at the edge of town and advanced on foot. Colonel Grierson observed, "The dismounted men went through the village of Union Church by sheer weight. Whole picket-fences were torn up and overturned by a rush."

Finding no opposition in the village, the troopers remounted and continued skirmishing with the Confederates as they drove them away from the town. The brigade bivouacked in town, waiting for the return of Captain Trafton's expedition. Only one trooper had been wounded in the day's fight. Colonel Grierson set the troopers in battle formation, prepared for the next wave of attack. That Confederate charge was the brigade's first real action since leaving La Grange eleven days earlier. It would not be the last: Grierson was certain of that.

Captain Stephen B. Cleveland led the Confederate charge at Union Church. With a detachment of 150 troopers, he was responsible for the defense of Natchez. Following General Pemberton's telegraphed orders, Cleveland rode east from Natchez to intercept the raiders. His ill-advised charge on Grierson's camp proved that he was outnumbered six-to-one. When nightfall ended the day's skirmishing, Captain Cleveland sent a mounted courier for reinforcements.

Cleveland's superior officer, Colonel William Wirt Adams, had left Grand Gulf the night before in search of Grierson. Adams had divided his troops with the idea of getting behind Grierson's brigade with a small detachment and driving the Yankees westward into an ambush.

Adams was the most dangerous opponent Colonel Grierson expected to face. He and Grierson had squared off in two battles the year before. Grierson respected Adams's fighting nature; Yankee soldiers fighting in the west called his troopers "a bunch of wild riders." Riding toward Adams's Grand Gulf headquarters, Grierson knew it was inevitable that the two would trade wits, if not shots, before the raid ended.

Near midnight of the twenty-eighth, Adams changed plans. As they closed in on Grierson's camp, Adams's scouts ascertained that they were vastly outnumbered by the Federals. Adams, then east of Union Church, needed to place all his men on the west side of that village and to form a defensive line with Captain Cleveland. First, he detached a lieutenant and two troopers to stay in the roadway and alert reinforcements from the east of his plans. Adams then flanked around Union Church and joined Captain Cleveland. Leaving his troops there, he rode with a few men to Fayette to assemble the rest of his regiment and retrace his steps to Union Church. With good luck, he would unleash a withering ambush on the unsuspecting Grierson the next afternoon.

As Grierson's luck would have it, Sergeant Richard Surby

led the "reinforcements" who happened upon Adams's left-behind lieutenant. Surby and his Butternut Guerrillas were scouting ahead of Trafton's detachment; they had made a feint at Bahala earlier and were returning to the brigade. Surby approached strangers warily at night, right hand on his revolver "for easy use." The Federal scout convinced the Confederate officer that he was part of a Mississippi Cavalry regiment searching for Adams. Surby and the hapless lieutenant continued:

> *"I reckon we can rest our guns, boys," said the lieutenant. "All right. We belong to old Wirt Adams' cavalry. And tomorrow we're goin' to give the Yanks hell."*
>
> *Surby asked, "Is Colonel Adams nearby?"*
>
> *"Colonel Adams went up to Fayette to get reinforcements. He left me behind to tell anybody coming up just to camp here till morning. He's aimin' to fix up ambush for the Yankees on yonder side of Union Church."*
>
> *"Ambush?"*
>
> *"That's right. If the Yankees think they're goin' to make Natchez, they're sure goin' to get slipped up."*

After "approving" Adams's plan, Surby went back to "get his colonel" and returned with enough men to capture the Confederates. Captain Trafton doubled the march pace immediately. His detachment reached Union Church before dawn and told Grierson its news. With this information, Grierson could steer his troopers once again away from disaster. Word of Surby's friendly interrogation spread quickly through camp at dawn; he was heartily congratulated. The troopers recognized how vital their Butternut Guerrillas were. Surby wrote:

*C.S.A. Colonel William Wirt Adams, First Mississippi Cavalry. He and
Colonel Robert V. Richardson pursued Grierson's brigade relentlessly.*
U.S. ARMY MILITARY HISTORY INSTITUTE

"I thought of the delay I had occasioned the column so many
times . . . how they must have cursed me, but they were igno-
rant of the proceeding in front, and as the prisoners continued
to be sent back they began to realise the importance of the
scouts, and their show of gratitude toward myself and com-
rade afterward has more than repaid me for the risk incurred."

Of course, the other side was also collecting intelligence.
This article appeared that morning, April 28, in the Jackson
Appeal:

From various sources, we have particulars of the enemy's movements from the north line of Mississippi, through the eastern portion of the State, almost to the Louisiana line. The route chosen for this daring dash was through the line of counties lying between the Mobile and Ohio, and New Orleans, Jackson and Great Northern railroads, in which, as they anticipated, there was no organized force to oppose them.

The penetration of an enemy's country, however, so extensively, will be recorded as one of the gallant feats of the war, no matter whether the actors escape or are captured. The expedition, we learn, was under command of Col. Grierson, of Illinois, who has already acquired considerable reputation as a dashing leader in West Tennessee. He boasted that he had no fears of his ability to extricate his command from the dangerous position it seemed to be in, but gave no indication as to the route he should take to get out of the country . . .

Whether they will move thence to Natchez . . . can only be conjectured; but we still incline to the opinion so confidently expressed some days ago, on first being advised of their presence at Newton, that Baton Rouge will be their haven, if undisturbed.

General Pemberton still had no clear idea what goal the raiders had. He had previously moved troops north of Jackson to intercept the Federals there. He had arrayed troops to block their movements east toward Alabama and northeast toward Tennessee. This day he ordered General Gardner at Port Hudson to take two different measures: block the road to Natchez and block southern exit routes to Baton Rouge. Captain Robert C. Love, who had been deceived and misdirected two days earlier by Corporal Samuel Nelson, finally checked in at

Hazlehurst. Pemberton ordered Love to round up all available cavalry and connect with Adams: "Hire horses and citizens and act promptly."

Throughout the day orders flew across the wires from Jackson. Pemberton gave Adams command of all cavalry in the area, along with the sole responsibility for stopping Grierson. He ordered the evacuation of an infantry training camp at Brookhaven, twenty-two miles south of Hazlehurst. He warned the commander that Grierson could be on his way.

Pemberton took time to wire reassuring news to General John Bowen at Grand Gulf: "Have reason to believe enemy are striking for Natchez or Baton Rouge." Pemberton was stunned by Bowen's reply: "Transports and barges loaded down with troops are landing at Hard Times, on the [Mississippi River's] west bank." A fierce artillery barrage from Union Admiral David Porter's gunboat squadron accompanied Grant's troop movement. Porter's cannon lobbed shells at Grand Gulf until dusk.

Apparently, Pemberton had lost sight of the fact that Grant was the real threat, just as Grant had hoped.

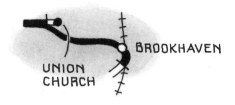

BROOKHAVEN
UNION
CHURCH

DAY THIRTEEN: WEDNESDAY, APRIL 29

With the railroad we did play "whack,"
Burning the cars upon the track;
We'd march all day and then all night,
And only stop to have a fight.
The people thought it very strange,
To see so many from La Grange;
They looked with wonder and surprise,
To see so many from Illinois.

That's one chorus of a song Sergeant Richard Surby composed after the attack on Newton Station; some of the raiders may have sung it on the road that day. Singing relieved boredom and released tension. Nobody had enough jokes or interesting stories to fill the endless hours the troopers clopped along dusty roads or snaked through deep forests and swamps.

Singing or not, the brigade was in motion by six that morning. Grierson continued to alter his plans according to circumstance. Going toward Grand Gulf, he faced the planned ambush uncovered by Surby. The renewed sounds of artillery shells exploding near Grand Gulf convinced him that General

Grant was not landing yet. Grierson said: "I had previously hoped to join General Grant in the vicinity of Grand Gulf or Port Gibson, yet the heavy firing from the gun boats heard by us satisfied me that it would be impracticable to undertake to do so, as it was very evident he had not at that time effected a landing with his troops. To delay an indefinite time to effect a junction would be too hazardous with my small command, in view of the large forces—over 20,000 men—sent out from various points to intercept and destroy us."

Consciously trying to out-think his opponents, Grierson decided they would least expect his brigade to backtrack east toward the New Orleans & Jackson Railroad. After all, he had struck the road twice already—at Hazlehurst and Bahala. Going east, back into the stronghold of the enemy, was the best option.

Grierson took steps to camouflage the plan. The Sixth Illinois marched west toward Fayette, ordered to make a strong demonstration toward William Wirt Adams's ambush. The Seventh Illinois followed for a distance, and then plunged into the oak forest that ringed Union Church. Making a wide loop that avoided Union Church, the Seventh finally aimed for Brookhaven.

To sow as much confusion as possible, Grierson staged a brief "play" before the march. As usual, numerous prominent citizens were at his temporary headquarters. When any town was secured, locals were detained for questioning and to ensure they did not ride off to inform before the brigade could leave. That morning, Grierson had a guard let one such person stand unnoticed in the colonel's temporary office. Stephen Forbes observed that "this gentleman . . . was permitted to overhear conversations and orders, made merely to deceive him, all implying a march for Natchez the next morning; and later a guard, instructed to be negligent, permitted him to slip away and escape."

On the way to Brookhaven it was evident that no combination of tricks could shelter the brigade much longer. Dozens of armed riders were seen observing the column's march before escaping into the woods; five were captured. The countryside was thick with oak and magnolia trees—perfect cover for an ambush. The path to Brookhaven switched back on itself several times. "I do not think we missed traveling toward any point of the compass," Surby said.

As the Sixth and Seventh were moving in opposite directions that morning—east and west—a new pursuer was zeroing in on them from the north. He was Colonel Robert V. Richardson. General Pemberton had given him command of the Twentieth Mississippi Mounted Infantry Regiment the night before. That appointment demonstrated just how desperate Pemberton was; Richardson was a wanted man.

General Hurlbut, Grierson's superior, had issued an arrest order declaring Richardson a war criminal and ordering his court-martial if captured. Worse, Pemberton's superior, General Joseph E. Johnston, had also issued an arrest order. Richardson stood accused of bribe-taking and intimidation of civilians. A week earlier, Pemberton himself had sent men to arrest Richardson for different violations of military law. Two weeks before Grierson's raid began, the Sixth and Seventh Illinois Cavalry had met Richardson's troopers in combat near Memphis, Tennessee. So many of Richardson's troopers were wounded and captured that Richardson abandoned his com-

mand and fled across the Mississippi in a canoe. All he took
was a bagful of money stolen from local citizens.

But when Richardson showed up in Jackson on April 28,
Pemberton gave him a new command instead of locking him
up. Richardson was an aggressive commander with a personal
grudge; he would hunt Grierson down.

Richardson was ordered to take his mounted infantry to Hazlehurst by train. He met his new command at 9 p.m., just the
beginning of a long night:

"When I got to the depot," Richardson's official report said,

*I was chagrined and surprised to find that the three companies
of the Twentieth Mississippi Mounted Infantry, who were to
constitute a portion of the forces subject to my orders in the
movement projected against the enemy, with horses, were just
beginning to be placed on the train.*

*About 2:30 a.m., April 29, 1863, the men and horses were
all aboard. I inquired for the conductor, and learned that he
was in bed at his chamber. I sent him an order to get up and
proceed with his train immediately, or I would send for him a
file of men. After a short time, he came. He then inquired of the
engineer whether he could pull the train, who replied that he
could not, because there were too many cars in the train.*

*The conductor and engineer then said that three cars must be
taken from the train. This was done. Now they said they had
not wood enough to run the train to the next station, and they
had no lamps. I inquired whether or not they had an ax to cut
wood; they replied they had none. About daybreak they started
with the train, and did not reach Hazlehurst until 11 a.m. In
spite of all efforts, these men were churlish, and seemed to be
laboring to defeat as far as possible the movement of troops.*

When he finally detrained at Hazlehurst, Richardson was as-
saulted with conflicting stories about Grierson's course: "He
was reported to have been that Tuesday morning at Union
Church . . . So far as I could judge, he was leaving the line of
the railroad and was going to Natchez . . . It seemed that the
proper direction for me to go . . . was Union Church."

By that time, the Sixth and Seventh had rejoined and were
approaching Brookhaven, twenty-two miles south of Hazlehurst. Surby reported back having scanned the area from a
wooded promontory above the town. Between two hundred
and three hundred armed men were milling around its streets.
Beyond the town lay a military camp with rows of wooden
barracks and tents neatly aligned. Grierson divided the regiments and deployed them for simultaneous charges on the
town and the camp.

The fury of men on horseback worked its effect on the town
guard. "There was much running and yelling but it soon qui-
eted down into almost a welcome," Grierson commented. The
military camp, practically deserted, gave way just as easily.
Pemberton had ordered this camp evacuated two days before,
just in case Grierson found it. Unfortunately, the trainee soldiers had not gone very far. Squads from the Sixth fanned out
in the woods, capturing cluster after cluster of Confederate
soldiers.

Before long, 216 soldiers were lined up on Brookhaven's
main street—all had to be paroled. Writing out parole papers
for each prisoner would be a day's work for the brigade's two
adjutants, but the effort and delay were worthwhile. Every
soldier paroled became a harmless, unarmed citizen again.
To Surby's surprise, people volunteered to become prisoners:
"Several citizens were hiding themselves in the woods, and as

soon as they learned that we were not destroying private property came into town, urgently requesting that they be paroled, so as to avoid the conscription."

The rest of the brigade did wrecking work. Companies were dispatched to rip up track, burn trestlework, and burn the army camp. In Brookhaven, the railroad station, freight cars, and a bridge were all set aflame. Once again the fire spread too far and houses took fire. This time, Grierson personally directed efforts to save civilian property. Sergeant Forbes led one fire-fighting team: "Our own soldiers climbed to the roofs of the houses and kept them wet by pouring water over them until the fire had burned down."

By this time, mid-afternoon, William Wirt Adams had conceded defeat. His entire regiment had awaited the Yankees since dawn on the Natchez road. Certain that he had been tricked, he wired for General Pemberton's permission to follow Grierson toward Baton Rouge. Colonel Richardson arrived in Union Church much later, about nine in the evening, and learned of the day's events. Grierson had headed for Brookhaven; Adams had been tricked again and was in pursuit again.

Richardson did not ask Pemberton's advice. He sent a courier to order Adams to meet him at Liberty, a town southwest of Brookhaven. Richardson and his mounted infantry took the nearest road south, parallel to Adams's path.

General Gardner, commanding at Port Hudson, was fed up with Grierson. He dispatched a very large force to catch the mischievous raiders. Colonel William R. Miles, with two thousand infantrymen, three hundred cavalrymen, and a battery of artillery, was sent east to hold the road at Clinton, Louisiana. Gardner also sent Major James De Baun with the Ninth Louisiana Partisan Rangers to hold the road at Woodville, Mississippi. Gardner was confident that Grierson could not escape past Miles and De Baun.

Grierson's brigade marched south from Brookhaven at dusk and settled for the night on a plantation eight miles from town. Uncertain of his next move, the colonel was content that the day was a success. The raiders had, Grierson wrote, "broke[n] up the railroad connection between Port Hudson and Vicksburg and rendered the rebel strongholds unable to communicate with, or support each other, besides starving them out by cutting off their supplies."

He might have wanted to make a spectacular dash toward the booming guns at Grand Gulf or possibly toward the safety of Baton Rouge. No dash was possible; it was beyond the endurance of his men and their animals. As Surby wrote that night, "For the first time in thirty-eight hours did a portion of the command take the saddles off their horses, and obtain time to sleep."

News of Grierson's achievement at Newton Station reached Grant that night. It brightened an otherwise frustrating day. Grant's gunboats had shelled the high cliffs of Grand Gulf relentlessly but could not damage the Confederate guns there. "I had about 10,000 troops on board transports and in barges alongside ready to land them and carry the place by storm the moment the batteries bearing on the river were silenced, so as to make the landing practicable," Grant wrote. The general's determination was inflexible, but his mind was adaptable. He had abandoned the plan to storm Grand Gulf by midafternoon; it was too well defended. He switched objectives and picked a new landing spot.

Admiral Porter's gunboats faced Grand Gulf's cannon again

that night. They exchanged fire with the big Confederate guns while the unarmed troop transports slipped downriver and out of range. Grant would land his infantrymen in the swamps south of Grand Gulf and hope that no rebel cavalry and mounted infantry would be waiting to pick them off.

BROOKHAVEN

BOGUE CHITTO

SUMMIT

DAY FOURTEEN: THURSDAY, APRIL 30

Before reveille blew for the raiders, Admiral Porter's gunboats resumed shelling the lofty fortress of Grand Gulf. On General Grant's signal, one gunboat drifted downstream. Once out of sight, it sped downriver to meet the troop barges. Taking the point, the gunboat steamed toward the eastern bank of the Mississippi. Behind its cover, the barges— loaded with thousands of infantrymen—churned slowly across the water. Near the shore, the gunboat lobbed shells randomly to break up the expected waiting party. But there was none.

The infantrymen waded to shore, and no shots were fired. That day, nearly ten thousand soldiers landed without a shot fired. Another thirteen thousand would follow. After months of setbacks and failures, the ground assault against Vicksburg was under way. General Sherman, with nearly seventeen thousand men, was moving toward Vicksburg from northern Mississippi. The Union was encircling the "Gibraltar of the Confederacy" at last.

Fifty miles away, on Gill's plantation south of Brookhaven, Grierson knew that *he* was encircled. Had he known about the landing, it's likely he would have fought his way to Grand

Gulf; two regiments of cavalry would be invaluable to Grant. But it would be a day, maybe two, before news traveled to him. Standing still was too great a risk to take. And riding through the Confederate lines on the presumption that a landing had been made was an even greater risk. Grierson opted to move south and strike yet another station on the New Orleans & Jackson Railroad.

As the brigade formed, its host gave the troopers words of praise and warning he later repeated to a newspaper writer: "Well, boys, I can't say I have anything against you. You haven't taken anything of mine except a little corn for your horses, and that you are welcome to. I've been hearing about you from all over the country. You're doing the boldest thing ever done. But you'll be trapped, though, you'll be trapped, mark me."

Their next stop was Bogue Chitto. Grierson ordered its train depot burned. A detachment went south and burned two railroad bridges. This was the fourth section of the New Orleans & Jackson Railroad the raiders had devastated. The damage was so great that it was not repaired until after the war. The raid had severed a vital supply line.

Rather than stopping for lunch, Grierson ordered a forced march to the next railroad junction, Summit. The brigade alternated between trotting and galloping under a brilliant midday sun. The heat and humidity of southern Mississippi must have grown increasingly uncomfortable. The Federal troopers were dressed in layers of heavy woolen clothes they had not washed or changed in two weeks.

Meanwhile, Colonel Richardson was in hot pursuit. On the road to Brookhaven he intercepted the unlucky Captain Robert C. Love's growing force. Love, who had been tricked by

Grierson's misdirections twice already, had followed General Pemberton's most recent orders. He hired horses and recruited riders in Hazlehurst.

Richardson attached Love's contingent to his mounted infantry as an advance unit. At Brookhaven they found smoldering ruins and no certain intelligence about Grierson's path. Richardson acted on the presumption that the Federals had continued southward: "After I had ordered Captain Love, as my advance, to proceed to Bogue Chitto, I received information that the enemy had committed his depredations there in the forenoon, and had gone on to Summit, to do the same thing, that evening." Convinced that the raiders could be caught the next day, Richardson dispatched a courier to locate William Wirt Adams and direct his regiment to Summit. Richardson, Love, and Adams would combine to outnumber Grierson's brigade.

Grierson's sense of urgency diminished that day, even as his pursuers quickened their pace. Reaching Summit at noon, he found no hint of armed resistance, quite the opposite. "There were no signs of excitement or fear displayed . . . They had received a favorable report of our behavior at Brookhaven, and Col. Grierson was almost as much of a favorite with them as General Pemberton," Surby noted. Grierson thought there was "much Union sentiment" and was grateful his men "were kindly welcomed and fed by many of the citizens."

Friendly faces and kind words must have been cheering after weeks in enemy territory. Still, the raiders had duties to perform. Search parties uncovered large quantities of Confederate army cornmeal, sugar, and molasses that were loaded onto empty freight cars before the cars were burned. Grierson spared the train depot, though. It was too near private buildings.

After bloodlessly crossing the Mississippi, Grant marched northeast and captured Jackson. Pemberton's force retreated into Vicksburg, and Grant commenced a siege of the city on May 22, illustrated here. General Pemberton finally surrendered both his army and the city on July 4, 1863.
LIBRARY OF CONGRESS

The brigade stayed in Summit far longer than necessary. While Grierson talked with residents, scouts were riding the countryside hunting for information. The news he got was inconclusive. There was no word of events at Grand Gulf; there were no positive sightings of his pursuers.

While the brigade lingered, the men got up to some mischief that agitated Grierson severely. They discovered thirty barrels of homemade rum hidden in a swamp beyond the town limits. "It was too late to save my men," he recalled in his autobiography. A detail was chosen that "emptied the vile stuff as remorselessly as I did the canteens of whiskey of my soldiers at Shawneetown, Illinois, two years before." Grierson could not afford to have light-headed troopers now; he had made a decision.

"Hearing nothing more of our forces at Grand Gulf and not being able to ascertain anything definite about General Grant's movements or whereabouts, I concluded to make for Baton Rouge," Grierson said. He sounded a general inspection. All ammunition was counted and redistributed equally. The worst horses were cut out and left behind. It was discovered that three troopers were absent during the inspection, men who had been present earlier in the day. Grierson counted them as stragglers. There was no time to look for them.

Having subtly planted the notion in people's minds that the Federals were going to attack the railroad at Osyka next, Grierson marched his troopers south. When the brigade was miles from town, it turned onto a back road headed west. Before leaving Summit, Grierson had secretly issued this command to his senior officers: "A straight line for Baton Rouge, and let speed be our safety!"

Not even Surby, scouting ahead of the column, knew its true

direction: "We were not more than one hundred miles from New Orleans. Were we going there? That was the question." The truth was, they were heading toward Liberty—the town where William Wirt Adams was waiting for them.

But Adams had tired of waiting in Liberty. Hearing about Grierson's railroad raids to the east, he ignored Richardson's command and marched toward Summit. Richardson, meanwhile, had marched south from Brookhaven in mid-afternoon, "hoping to be able to find the enemy encamped [at Summit] or in the vicinity, and determined to make a night attack." Captain Love, leading Richardson's advance party, traveled all the way to Bogue Chitto and captured Grierson's three stragglers. They were questioned at length, but honestly could not reveal Grierson's objective beyond Summit.

By the time Richardson and Love reached the outskirts of Summit, they had become convinced, by rumors, that the Federals were camping for the night in Summit. They halted too far from town to see the rear guard of Grierson's brigade leaving at that moment. Richardson stopped north of town to rest and prepare for a predawn surprise attack.

More Confederates were in motion that night elsewhere; word of Grierson's plan to raid Osyka spread rapidly. Major De Baun, waiting in Woodville, was ordered to race to Osyka's rescue. Traveling half the distance, he rested in Liberty, the town Adams had evacuated earlier. Another Confederate Commander heard of the rumored attack fifty miles south of Osyka in Ponchatoula, Louisiana. Not waiting for orders, he force-marched an infantry regiment and cavalry company to the endangered railroad depot.

For the first time in more than a week, General John Pemberton issued no orders concerning Grierson's raid. The ruckus in his backyard was nothing compared with the unwelcome visitors marching toward his front porch.

At day's end, Richardson and Adams were uncomfortably close to the raiders. Grierson camped at a plantation fifteen miles west of Richardson. Adams camped less than five miles west of Grierson. The raiders were weary and hungry and dirty. They must have expected that a major battle was unavoidable. *All* their spirits were still high if this story of the colonel's is true:

There had been all these fourteen days of hard work and scanty rest and rations, wherein the officers had scarcely fared better than the men; at least the men were always first served. This night I was determined that my staff and I should have a good supper. I accordingly stationed a guard at the well-filled chicken coop, while the smokehouses and store-houses were opened as usual, and their contents dealt out to the men.

But perhaps the Louisiana rum was not yet worked off—I was suddenly made aware that the men . . . were devastating that chicken coop. I looked in, and saw the last chicken, and a hand grasping for it. Saber in hand, I went for that private. Over the hen coop, around the pig-sty, through the stable, behind the smokehouses, between the horses, and under the horses, dodging the trees, and jumping the briers, down the steps, and smashing the trellis—the hen squawking, I vociferating, the laughing officers cheering the novel chase, till over a picket fence went the soldier, dropping the fowl under my saber. It did not require much picking by this time, but I had earned my fricassee.

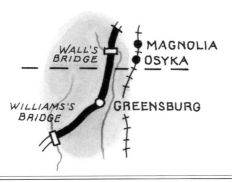

DAY FIFTEEN: FRIDAY, MAY 1

The day was dazzlingly sunny. "A gentle breeze floated through the trees," remembered Sergeant Surby, "causing a rustling among the green leaves of the oaks. Perched among the branches was the mocking bird, singing a variety of notes, the whole impressing the beholder with a sense of a Creator of all this beauty . . . We little dreamed what a change would be produced in a few hours."

For a full two weeks, Colonel Grierson's brigade glided through the heart of enemy territory. The troopers had worked almost flawlessly as a team. The colonel's deceptive strategy was informed by the intelligence gathered by cunning and brave scouts. The main column marched and worked together with dedication. When ordered, the soldiers charged with abandon. The brigade had inflicted massive physical damage on the Confederacy; it had suffered unbelievably little damage to itself. One trooper had been killed during its long march. Three troopers had been left under a doctor's care. Six were listed as missing, probably captured.

But Grierson expected a reckoning. He may have thought

there was no way to avoid a clash—so many Confederates were in pursuit. "Three more rivers were yet to be crossed; the enemy were gathering thick and fast behind us and we were near their strongholds," he wrote. The Tickfaw was the first river; Wall's Bridge was the objective.

Lieutenant Colonel William Blackburn volunteered to lead the advance. "I charged him *particularly* to make a cautious advance," Grierson wrote later. Speaking personally to Surby, Grierson said, "Let nothing escape your observation on either side of the road. If you see anything suspicious, report back to me at once. And don't get more than half a mile from the advance." The scouts normally kept two miles or more ahead of the column. Grierson wanted a tight formation, ready to react instantly to attack. Surby thought, "It was not the intention of Colonel Grierson to engage the enemy, but rather avoid him. I am satisfied of one thing—that had we been compelled to fight it would have been a desperate one."

They marched southwest through thick woods dotted by cultivated fields. Grierson sent two detachments to make feints at the railroad junctions of Magnolia and Osyka. At ten that morning the scouts crossed the main road linking Liberty and Osyka. "I at once discovered by the newly-made tracks, that a column had passed, and could not have been long before," Surby said. Colonel Grierson came forward to read the tracks. All agreed that a Confederate force was on the way to Wall's Bridge.

Major De Baun's three cavalry companies had made the tracks. After camping at Liberty the night before, De Baun was marching to Osyka. Osyka was the raiders' next stop, according to De Baun's commander, General Gardner. Around noon, De Baun's troopers stopped to rest and water their horses at

Wall's Bridge. De Baun sent pickets back to protect his column. Hungry themselves, the Confederate pickets stopped at a plantation half a mile from the bridge. Surrounded by a thick oak forest, the plantation house was hidden from the road. A long, sharply angled gravel driveway led from the road to the house. Seven Confederate troopers rode up to the house in search of food; the remaining three stayed at the roadside.

Surby and his scouts, traveling single file for safety, passed out of the woods and saw the same white plantation house surrounded by forest. Coming to the driveway's entrance, they encountered the three Confederate pickets. Surby made conversation with the rebels, learning that they had "been traveling night and day after the d——d Yanks." Before learning any more, he heard two shots fired in the distance, followed by rifle fire.

The advance company of the Seventh regiment had come through the forest from a different direction and found a second driveway entrance to the plantation. That drive was also winding and shielded by rows of poplar and oak. Although they were separated by only four hundred yards, Surby and the advance company could not see each other. Lieutenant James Gaston of the Seventh led a dozen troopers up the second driveway to investigate.

"As they [Gaston's platoon] rode up to the gate," Surby said, "they were surprised at seeing four armed rebels standing around in the yard . . . the 'rebs' were surprised as well, and both parties showed a disposition to fight." The Confederates fired first, wounding one raider. Gaston drew his saber, and the platoon charged. Two Confederates were captured, and two escaped into the thick woods.

This skirmish produced immediate action on both sides. At Wall's Bridge, De Baun ordered his men and horses to take cover in the woods encircling the bridge. "I immediately ordered the bridge to be dismantled and the men ambushed," De Baun wrote in his formal report, "posting men at the bridge to destroy it as soon as the rear guard would have reported." When the rear guard—the pickets fighting outside the plantation house—failed to report ten minutes later, De Baun sent an officer back "to ascertain, if possible, the cause of the delay."

When the skirmish began, Surby moved into action: "Giving my scouts the sign, each of us covered his man with a revolver and ordered them to surrender and raise their hands over their heads, or he would fire." The new prisoners were being sent back as Lieutenant Colonel Blackburn rode up to Surby, questioned the scout, and told him to resume the lead—cautiously.

Minutes later, the scouts intercepted two Confederates coming down the road. It was a captain and his orderly sent to reconnoiter by De Baun. Surby promptly deceived the Confederates, and they surrendered.

Before the captured officer could be interrogated, Blackburn rode forward eagerly: "Sergeant! Bring along your scouts and follow me, and I'll see where those rebels are hiding!" Without stopping for discussion, Blackburn trotted beyond his scouts. "It seemed to me," Surby wrote, "that this was a rash movement on the part of Colonel Blackburn, but he had ordered me to follow him, and it was my duty to obey."

The lane leading to Wall's Bridge was shady and deeply forested on each side; the river was not visible. "That a force was down in the bottom, and that was not very far off, was pretty well understood; but what that force was, and their number, we did not know . . . as the game says, we had to 'go it blind.' "

When Blackburn's small party reached Wall's Bridge, the area was deserted. The side railings of the narrow structure had been taken apart, but the floor was intact. They saw nobody across the span—only deep woods yards from the opposite side. Blackburn had begun crossing the bridge when a single shot was fired, followed immediately by dozens more. "It seemed as though a flame of fire burst forth from every tree," Surby said. De Baun's Confederates were shooting from the woods.

Blackburn's horse was hit and fell on the lieutenant colonel. Surby was rushing ahead to help when he felt intense pain and heat in his side; he had been shot in the thigh. The bridge was blocked by another scout's fallen horse; the scout was using his dead horse for cover and firing into the woods. Surby saw blood rushing from Blackburn's head. Afraid of losing consciousness, Surby spurred his horse away from the bridge, dismounted, and fell down. He felt blood seeping through his pant leg into his boot.

In the same moment, Lieutenant William H. Styles, with Company G of the Seventh Illinois, galloped past Surby toward the bridge. The troopers had crossed the bridge without resistance when the Confederates unleashed a volley from the woods. Seven horses went down immediately. Confederates rushed from the woods, and Styles wisely ordered retreat. Styles and three troopers made their escape across the bridge. Three men were shot; five were captured by De Baun. If De Baun's Mississippi troopers had carried repeating rifles, almost certainly all Styles's troopers and all the scouts would have been slaughtered near Wall's Bridge. The Mississippians charged after the first volley rather than taking time to reload.

Lieutenant Colonel Blackburn had acted recklessly—there was no reason for his small party to cross the apparently un-guarded bridge. Styles's crossing in the face of a hidden enemy force had been even more reckless. Both paid a heavy price.

After Styles's retreat, Colonel Grierson rode up, leading two companies of the Seventh. As Grierson shouted orders, the companies dismounted and formed up in columns facing the bridge. Captain Jason Smith rolled up with one of his small Woodruff guns. When the cannon commenced firing into the woods, De Baun's troopers returned rifle fire, and then stopped. The muzzle flashes in the woods gave Smith a target. A second cannon joined the first moments later. The Sixth reg-iment arrived. Grierson ordered a battalion to cross the bridge, single file, past the fallen Blackburn. The two remaining bat-talions of the Sixth went up- and downstream to ford the river. The Seventh, fanned out opposite the camouflaged Con-federates, gave covering fire.

As the Federals crossed, De Baun was already in disorderly retreat. Shaken by the cannonade, his Mississippi partisans fled, leaving a trail of blankets, coats, and rifles behind. In his official report, De Baun said, "My command being small . . . and fearing to be surrounded, I ordered a retreat in the direc-tion of Osyka."

Grierson sent the Sixth regiment in pursuit of the rebels while the Seventh dealt with casualties. Colonel Grierson and his staff had to consider the brigade's options after the attack. What direction was the next wave of Confederates coming from? Grierson would have been relieved if he had known what Richardson and Adams were up to that day.

At 3 a.m., Richardson's troops charged into Summit with orders to fire at will. "We . . . learned that the enemy had left about sunset on the previous evening," Richardson said, "marching on the road to Magnolia . . . saying he intended to go to that place; thence to Osyka." Colonel Richardson was convinced. Magnolia housed a tannery, and Osyka had an important warehouse filled with military supplies.

Richardson started his troops on an end run: "I hoped to be able by taking a road east of the railroad to get in his front, and form an ambuscade." At sunrise, his troops were in place, the ambush ready. A scout sent to determine Grierson's eastward progress returned hours later with distressing news. Rumor had it that Grierson was marching west instead.

Richardson refused to believe he had been duped by Grierson. "My men and horses had marched all night," he later wrote in his official report to headquarters. "I remained three hours to feed and rest, when I marched for Magnolia, hoping to be able by another night march to overtake and attack the enemy at or near Osyka."

William Wirt Adams still hoped to combine his forces with Richardson's but had been unable to locate him. A courier from Adams reached Richardson that morning and returned with instructions to join forces at Magnolia. Adams had second thoughts, though, during his march to Magnolia. He received convincing intelligence that Grierson's raiders were heading straight to Baton Rouge with no thought of turning east to raid the railroad again.

Adams could not bring himself to switch course again, but did take a precaution. He dispatched a lone rider, Lieutenant W. S. Wren, to gallop forty miles and burn Williams's Bridge on the Amite River. The Amite was the second of the three rivers Grierson had to cross. If Williams's Bridge were destroyed, the raiders would have no escape route. Grierson would be forced to turn east and run, eventually, into the outstretched arms of Adams and Richardson.

As Adams and Richardson pushed tired troops forward to a showdown at Magnolia or Osyka or somewhere else, Grierson assessed the damage caused by De Baun's ambush. Five men were captured; three were wounded during Styles's charge. Lieutenant Colonel Blackburn and Sergeant Surby were seriously wounded. A wagon was lined with blankets and used as an ambulance; the wounded were carried to a plantation across the Tickfaw River.

Before his wound was treated, Surby was stripped of his Butternut Guerrilla disguise dressed in uniform. He was unable to ride and would be taken prisoner. Grierson did not want him hanged as a spy—the almost universal penalty for impersonating your enemy in wartime. Surby had the presence of mind to give his diary of the raid to a friend; he wanted that to survive even if he did not.

Even though Blackburn's wounds were mortal, he voiced his opinion during a hastily called council of officers. Blackburn advised pushing forward to Baton Rouge immediately. Grierson concurred. The colonel allowed the brigade's surgeon and two troopers to stay behind. In effect, they volunteered to become prisoners of war along with their wounded comrades.

Sergeant Surby experienced mixed emotions about the parting. "Many a kind farewell was given, and friends parted, some never to meet again on this side of the grave," he thought. He had regrets about the day's action: "Had Lieutenant Gaston and squad not entered the [plantation] house, thereby meeting the enemy, firing upon each other and giving the alarm, all would no doubt have ended well . . . Another sad mistake was that Lieut.-Colonel Blackburn, unfortunately with too much daring, proceeded across the bridge with no other support than a few scouts."

Grierson thanked the wounded men for their gallant actions but regretted that Blackburn was "not as discreet and wary as he was brave . . . The passage of the Tickfaw might have been a complete surprise and accomplished without loss but for the accident of the firing and alarm. Unfortunately, Lieutenant-Colonel Blackburn, calling on the scouts to follow him, dashed forward to the bridge without waiting for the column to come into supporting distance." Grierson regretted any loss of men, especially any unnecessary loss. Blackburn was a brave and val-

The advance of a cavalry skirmish line toward the enemy. LIBRARY OF CONGRESS

ued leader. He had led the raid of Newton Station, captured two enemy trains, and devastated the station.

Grierson's anger quickly cooled. Describing the bridge engagement days later in a report to General Grant's headquarters, Grierson wrote: "I cannot speak too highly of the bravery of the men upon this occasion, and particularly of Lieutenant-Colonel Blackburn, who, at the head of his men, charged upon the bridge, dashed over, and by undaunted courage, dislodged the enemy from his strong position."

The raiders were roughly fifty miles from the outskirts of Baton Rouge and safety. Grierson would not rest until they crossed Williams's Bridge: "The Amite River, a wide and rapid stream, was to be crossed, and there was but one bridge by which it could be crossed, and this was in exceedingly close proximity to Port Hudson. This I determined upon securing before I halted." That was a wise decision. General Gardner, commanding Port Hudson, had already received this message about the raiders: "To stop them at Williams' Bridge is the last chance."

Corporal Samuel Nelson, the trooper who diverted Confederate Captain Robert C. Love, was given command of the Butternut scouts. He guided them across the state line into Louisiana and to the town of Greensburg. Greensburg was not garrisoned and the troops passed through without incident. They continued traveling southwest without rest. There was no time even to water the horses.

Nelson and his scouts captured couriers with dispatches from General Gardner: all men under Gardner's command were ordered to Williams's Bridge at a gallop. Around midnight, they neared the bridge. Nelson was sent to inquire at neighboring homes about normal troop strength on the bridge.

Assured that it was guarded by a small detail at night, the column waited on a hill above the river while Nelson and another scout went to work. "The scouts advanced with letter in hand as couriers on the way to Port Hudson. A cocked revolver quickly placed at the heads of the guards, no words were spoken above a whisper and both were readily captured," Grierson wrote.

Grierson's two regiments passed routinely over the two-hundred-yard-long bridge minutes later. As Captain Forbes wrote, it could easily have been different:

We afterward learned that General Gardner commanding at Port Hudson, apprised of our approach, had correctly foreseen our destination and made his dispositions for our capture. He preferred not to burn the bridge, as he needed it for his own uses, but thought it better to meet and capture us at that point. Dispatching, therefore, an ample force of infantry and cavalry, accompanied by a battery of artillery, to command the bridge, he waited our arrival. His detachments marched through Clinton [Louisiana] and bivouacked for refreshment in the outskirts of the town. The good citizens, rejoiced at the foreseen capture of Grierson and his raiders, tendered a complimentary dance to the officers of the rebel command.

The officers had carefully estimated the time of our possible arrival near the bridge, and accepted the compliment as an incident too pleasant to be needlessly rejected. While, therefore, we were stretching our legs for the bridge, these gentlemen were stretching theirs in the cotillion. After they had danced they marched. After we had marched we danced—when we learned they arrived at the bridge just two hours after we had crossed it.

None of the raiders' other pursuers felt like dancing that night. Major De Baun reached Osyka before nightfall but found neither Richardson nor Adams. He bivouacked there and waited for the tireless Richardson. Richardson and his troopers arrived with bad news: "The enemy had not approached Osyka nearer than Wall's Bridge, but had gone on the road to Greensburg," he reported to Pemberton. Richardson attached De Baun's force, fed and rested his horses, and started for Greensburg, Louisiana, after midnight.

William Wirt Adams learned of the fight at Wall's Bridge near Magnolia and turned westward immediately. After crossing Wall's Bridge, he officially captured the wounded and the medical staff left behind near the bridge. Barely conscious, Lieutenant Colonel Blackburn assured Adams that Grierson had turned west and was marching toward the Mississippi. The legion of Colonel William R. Miles arrived at Wall's Bridge hours later. Surby said, "They felt confident of capturing the 'Yanks' and did not appear to be in any hurry, stating that a force had been sent out from Port Hudson, and that they would intercept our forces when they attempted to cross the Amite River." Had that force skipped the dance, they might have done it.

General Pemberton sent his last orders concerning Grierson's raid that evening. The orders to Colonel Richardson confirm that he clearly knew the source of his problem at last. "Instead of pursuing Grierson farther, your command will return in direction of Port Gibson, to operate against the enemy [Grant] there. If you can communicate with Colonel Wirt Adams, tell him same thing."

DAY SIXTEEN: SATURDAY, MAY 2

"We were over the Amite, and the worst crisis of the raid was past," Stephen Forbes wrote. "All the more heavily, as the excitement of danger died away, there settled down on the hearts of the raiders the overwhelming sense of hunger and fatigue. There were still some thirty miles to ride before we might halt to eat and rest, and I am sure that no one who rode them will ever forget that night."

Another day's march would put them inside their own lines. An attack by an enemy force could come at any minute. And those attackers might be less sleepy, less hungry, and equipped with fresher horses. Knowing the stakes did not make the march any easier. Captain Henry Forbes struggled to keep the troopers awake:

Men by the score, and I think by fifties, were riding sound asleep in their saddles. The horses excessively tired and hungry, would stray out of the road and thrust their noses to the earth in hopes of finding something to eat. The men, when addressed, would remain silent and motionless until a blow across the thigh or the shoulder should awaken them, when it would be found that each supposed himself still riding with his company, which might perhaps be a mile ahead. We found several men who had either fallen from their horses, or dismounted and dropped on the ground, dead with sleep. Nothing short of a beating with the flat of a saber would awaken some of them. In several instances they begged to be allowed to sleep, saying that they would run all risk of capture on the morrow. Two or three did escape our vigilance, and were captured the next afternoon.

Dawn brought a cloudless sky and blinding sun to make the men even sleepier. The Louisiana countryside—bayous of brackish water, Spanish moss draped over the trees, roads hemmed in by overgrowing vines and brambles—was dream-like itself.

At Sandy Creek, the scouts reported a nearly empty enemy camp guarding the creek's narrow bridge. Grierson ordered a charge on the camp, possibly just to wake the men up.

Two companies of the Sixth thundered across the bridge and took the camp without resistance. Forty Mississippi state troops were captured; they were all ill or wounded. The rest of the force had marched a day earlier to help defeat Grierson's raiders at Osyka. "Having destroyed the camp," Grierson reported, "consisting of about one hundred and fifty tents, a large quantity of ammunition, guns, public and private stores, books, papers, and public documents, I immediately took the road to Baton Rouge."

They pressed on through the heart of sugar-plantation country. Warned of the raiders' coming, the white owners and overseers were in hiding. But slaves were everywhere; most were eager to join the march. They knew that they were only miles away from freedom.

The raiders had varying impressions of African-Americans in bondage during their ride across the state of Mississippi. Kept as property, slaves were valued mostly for their labor. It was illegal for them to read and write, and they were almost completely dependent on their owners for news of the world beyond their plantations. What they were told was untrue.

"It was very amusing, sometimes, to witness the astonishment depicted on the faces of the negroes when they learned that we were Yankees. So many falsehoods had been told them by their masters and mistresses that we were a different people—ugly, deformed, and very wicked, that the poor slaves had conjured up in their minds a fearful picture," Sergeant Surby wrote. The slaves quickly formed new opinions after meeting the Yankees. Dozens provided valuable intelligence to Grierson's men; some served as guides. Hundreds tried to attach themselves to the brigade but fell behind. On foot or mule, they could not keep up with the furious pace.

Colonel Grierson, like most Northerners, had enlisted to help preserve the Union, not to promote the interests of slaveholders. In 1861 a general order of the U.S. Army directed commanders to return runaway slaves to their owners. Grierson said, "I determined to quit and go to my home before I would be forced into the position of a slave-catcher for the rebels of our country who were totally unworthy [of] such acts of conciliation when in open war and rebellion." The Emancipation Proclamation of 1863 changed everything. All slaves within the rebellious states were officially free. Because the sixteenth day's march was slow and its end was near, Grierson let slaves from the sugar plantations join the march toward Baton Rouge.

Hundreds of African-Americans formed a makeshift rear

guard for the brigade. They rode in lumber wagons and fancy carriages. They rode mules and walked. They drove oxen and carried chickens. They sang to celebrate their deliverance from bondage.

Riding advance, Corporal Nelson and his scouts encountered a lone Confederate officer around nine that morning. After warning the scouts that "the road's full of Yankees in our rear," the officer divulged that he was a member of Miles's legion— on his way to warn the rebels guarding the Comite River crossing. The Comite was the final river to be crossed.

After sending that prisoner back to the main column, Nel-

African-Americans leave the plow and the plantation behind to seek freedom under the protection of an advancing Union army. LIBRARY OF CONGRESS

son visited a farmhouse to share a few bites of food with a Confederate lieutenant stopping there. The lieutenant volunteered that the Comite River was guarded by one company of Confederates at the best fording place. Nelson and a fellow scout continued and found conditions at the river as expected.

When the brigade arrived, Grierson decided that a headlong sabers-drawn, trooper-screaming charge would be the most effective approach. A battalion of the Seventh deployed on two sides of the camp and charged it furiously. As often happened, the shock of the charge melted any resistance. The Confederate defenders had only seconds to form up in front of tons of galloping horseflesh and gleaming swords or to run. They ran, abandoning the camp and throwing down their weapons to run faster. The battalion eventually rounded up forty-two prisoners. Those prisoners, along with the others taken during the last day, were not paroled. They joined the lengthening line of march to Baton Rouge as prisoners of war.

They had crossed the last barrier, the Comite River. Grierson's map informed him that they were nine miles or less from the Federal picket lines guarding Baton Rouge. Assuming the brigade was out of harm's way, he ordered a rest halt a few miles forward. Grierson said rest and food, for men and horses, were imperative: "So tired they were, they scarcely waited for food before every man save two or three was in a profound slumber." Introducing himself to the plantation owner, the soldier-musician found a temptation he could not resist: "I astonished the occupants by sitting down and playing upon a piano . . . and in that manner I managed to keep awake, while my soldiers were enjoying themselves by relaxation, sleep and quiet rest." Unfortunately, the colonel never recorded what pieces he played to entertain himself and the brigade that day.

He did record some of his thoughts, though. "Only six miles then to Baton Rouge," Grierson wrote. "Think of the great relief to the overtaxed mind and nerves. I felt that we had nobly accomplished the work assigned to us and no wonder that I felt musical; who would not under like circumstances?"

The concert ended abruptly. Pickets rode in with news: Confederates were approaching from the west. Grierson did not rouse his exhausted troopers: "Feeling confident that no enemy could come against us from that direction, I rode out alone to meet the troops without waking up my command." Seeing that the supposed Confederates were dressed in blue, Grierson tried to approach, but "so cautious were they, with their skirmishers creeping along behind the fences," that Grierson waved a white handkerchief of truce and repeatedly called out his name and rank. The "Confederates" dismounted and hung back. Their captain "apparently was not at all satisfied with the looks of things," Grierson wrote. Eventually they approached each other, and "when we met and shook hands," Grierson said, "his soldiers sprang up and clambered onto the fence and gave a shout." The "Confederate" was actually Union Captain J. Franklin Godfrey, from Baton Rouge. He had a funny tale to tell.

When Grierson had called a rest halt earlier, one soldier had unwittingly pressed on. "One of my orderlies who happened to be asleep and therefore did not hear the order, went moping on nodding to the motion of the horse and the tired steed realizing that a town was near and a better resting place, walked on to the Federal picket line," Grierson later wrote. The orderly was captured by the Federal infantry guarding Baton Rouge and taken for questioning. Because his story was so improbable—that he was with Illinois cavalry from La Grange,

Tennessee—he was taken to General Christopher Augur, commander of Federal land forces in Baton Rouge. Augur refused to believe the story. Neither he nor General Nathaniel Banks at New Orleans knew anything about a cavalry raid from La Grange. None of Grierson's commanders, not even General Grant, had thought of telling Baton Rouge that the raiders might head there.

So Augur dispatched a cavalry company under Captain Godfrey with orders to "proceed cautiously" and "ascertain the truth." If Captain Godfrey needed more proof than Grierson's word and uniform, he got it when his company rode into Grierson's camp. "The [Confederate] prisoners were rather jubilant," Grierson said. "They twitted the [Federal] Baton Rouge soldiers that *they* couldn't take them, only ten miles off, and that the Union Army had to send a force all the way from Tennessee to take them in the rear."

Captain Godfrey sent a courier back to General Augur; the news ricocheted about town. "The inhabitants of Baton Rouge were startled by the arrival of a courier," a St. Louis newspaper reported, "who announced that a brigade of cavalry from General Grant's army had cut their way through the heart of rebel country . . . The information seemed too astounding for belief."

General Augur sent a detachment in full dress uniform to guide Grierson's raiders into the city. He intercepted the brigade outside town and insisted they enter on parade. Grierson claimed that his men were barely recognizable as Federal troopers; men and horses needed food and rest. But the parade took place anyway.

The line of march into Baton Rouge extended nearly two miles. The Sixth Illinois headed the procession. It was followed by Captain Smith's artillery unit, the Confederate pris-

The "triumphal procession" of the raiders into Baton Rouge. The picture is completely fanciful but was a wonderful morale builder for Northern civilians.

oners, the Seventh Illinois, and the led horses and mules. At the rear were more than three hundred freed slaves. One newspaper reporter noted that "singing, playing and shouting, they presented the most wonderful appearance imaginable."

The parade was a glorious end to a nearly impossible mission. Grierson said, "For half a mile before entering the city, the road was lined with wondering spectators, old and young, male and female, rich and poor, white and black, citizens and soldiers. Amidst shouts and cheers, and waving of banners, heralded by music, the tired troops marched around the public square, down to the river to water their horses, and then to Magnolia Grove, two miles south of the city."

The raiders were greeted by squadrons from Massachusetts and New York infantry regiments. The soldiers had volunteered to cook hot meals, but Grierson's exhausted troopers wanted rest more than food. For the first time in sixteen days, not a single trooper had sentry duty that night. They all slept, without fear, underneath sweet-smelling magnolia trees.

Colonel Grierson composed his summary report for General Hurlbut:

> *During the expedition* we *killed and wounded about one hundred of the enemy, captured and paroled over 500 prisoners, many of them officers, destroyed between fifty and sixty miles of railroad and telegraph, captured and destroyed over 3,000 stand of arms, and other army stores and Government property to an immense amount; we also captured 1,000 horses and mules.*
>
> *Our loss during the entire journey was 3 killed, 7 wounded, 5 left on the route sick; the sergeant-major and surgeon of the Seventh Illinois left with Lieutenant-Colonel Blackburn, and*

9 men missing, supposed to have straggled. We marched over 600 miles in less than sixteen days. The last twenty-eight hours we marched 76 miles, had four engagements with the enemy, and forded the Comite River, which was deep enough to swim many of the horses. During this time the men and horses were without food or rest.

Lieutenant Colonel Blackburn and a trooper wounded at the Wall's Bridge shootout died. Sergeant Surby and the wounded and sick troopers left behind survived.

FAMOUS!

⭐ "My dear Alice, I like Byron have had to wake up in the morning and find myself famous. Since I have been here it has been one continuous ovation. I have received 4 months pay today and enclosed you will find draft on New York [bank] for $500," Grierson wrote on May 6. The modest, reserved colonel could not deny the obvious—the boys from Illinois were famous, and they were heroes. The raid was just the boost Northern morale needed; the long season of doubt and despair was over. The superiority of the Southern horsemen was disproved—Grierson's raiders had bested them. The notion of unyielding resistance by Southerners had been exploded—"Grierson has knocked the heart out of the state," reported one Mississippian.

At first, the troopers just wanted to sleep and eat and get their feet accustomed to solid ground again. Stephen Forbes, in a letter to home, summed up the brigade's feelings: "Sleeping under a tent for the first time since April 17 . . . Unspeakable luxury to have a change of clean clothes, soft bread, and milk to eat, if you buy it. Morning papers and monthlies to read." Some troopers attended church services that day. Many stayed in Magnolia Grove—tending their horses, washing and mending their ragged uniforms, and just swapping stories.

Some men suffered post-traumatic stress, a delayed reaction to the harrowing experiences they had endured. Captain Henry Forbes, the unflappable commander of Company B, suffered a brief but total breakdown. "It was pathetically significant of the stress and strain of the long hard ride," Stephen Forbes told his family, "that he was taken with cautious violence to the post hospital, tearing the curtains from the ambulance on the way, and swearing that we might kill him if we would but we could never take him prisoner."

A few days later, Captain Forbes had recovered sufficiently to write home reassuringly:

> *I have risen refreshed this morning and have thrown open my windows and opened my paper to write you a letter . . . I suppose there is no need of telling you of our dare-devil expedition—our neck-or-nothing ride through the heart of Dixie, as I believe among all the startling events of the immediate past, that has made its own noise and secured its own record. The facts of our having performed the greatest march in a given time on record, you understand, the thousand and one incidents of it can only be talked up . . . I was once forty-eight hours without tasting food, and we rode at one time fifty-two miles without feeding. This was thought to be doing pretty well for one little company, and indeed my officers speak of it in terms too kind to bear repetition from me. We tried to do the best we could, and there was One who covered our defenseless heads. We had one man killed and had one wounded, though he rode bravely through for fully four hundred miles bearing two severe wounds. With such men you can accomplish what you will.*

Restaurants and bars offered those men free food and liquor for days on end. The city's outpouring of gratitude and goodwill eventually lured the troopers into rowdy behavior. After several pranks got out of hand, Grierson firmly reestablished proper discipline, but defended his men vigorously: "On finding themselves such privileged characters it was not strange they should indulge in some skylarking . . . All this disorder was but the effervescence of a few days."

Grierson did nothing to constrain the nation's effervescence. When news of the raid finally reached the North—communications from Louisiana were slow then—the floodgates of pride opened. On May 17, *The New York Times* devoted its front and back pages to the raid; other papers followed with equal coverage. Some wrote long series of articles tracking the raid's day-by-day progress. *Harper's Weekly* and *Frank Leslie's Illustrated Newspaper*—the *Time* and *Newsweek* of the nineteenth century—wrote lengthy stories enlivened by drawings re-creating aspects of the raid. Grierson's portrait appeared on the cover of both magazines; he was the informal "Man of the Year."

Grierson's superiors applauded the military importance of the raid. General Sherman called it "the most brilliant expedition of the war." After Vicksburg surrendered on July 4—the raid's larger goal—General Grant's official report on the campaign explained the raid's contribution. Grierson, he wrote, had undertaken "a raid through the central portion of the State of Mississippi, to destroy railroads and other public property, for the purpose of creating a diversion in favor of the army moving to the attack on Vicksburg. On April 17, this expedition started, and arrived at Baton Rouge on May 2, having successfully traversed the whole State of Mississippi. This ex-

HARPER'S WEEKLY.

JOURNAL OF CIVILIZATION.

Vol. VII.—No. 336.]   NEW YORK, SATURDAY, JUNE 6, 1863.   [SINGLE COPIES TEN CENTS. $3.00 PER YEAR IN ADVANCE.

Entered according to Act of Congress, in the Year 1863, by Harper & Brothers, in the Clerk's Office of the District Court for the Southern District of New York.

COLONEL GRIERSON, SIXTH ILLINOIS CAVALRY.—From a Photograph by Jacobs, of New Orleans.—[See Page 354.]

pedition was skillfully conducted, and reflects great credit on Colonel Grierson and all of his command. The notice given this raid by the Southern press confirms our estimate of its importance. It has been one of the most brilliant cavalry exploits of the war, and will be handed down in history as an example to be imitated."

And rewarded. Grierson was promoted to brigadier general and made chief of cavalry of Grant's Sixteenth Army Corps.

Grierson's commanders were not the only military men to recognize his contribution. When General Gardner surrendered the last Confederate stronghold on the Mississippi River, Port Hudson, he said: "Grierson caused the surrender of Port Hudson by cutting off communications and supplies." Gardner asked to meet Grierson after the capitulation. After Grant introduced Grierson, the Confederate officer theatrically waved a fistful of telegraph messages in the air and said: "Grierson was here; no, he was *there*, sixty miles away. He marched north, no, south, or again west . . . The trouble was, my men ambushed you where you did not go; they waited for you till morning while you passed by night."

But when the celebration finally ebbed, the war was far from over. The Sixth and Seventh Illinois, along with the Second Iowa, saw many more fights before General Lee surrendered in April 1865. Grierson personally commanded the Illinois regiments on another raid through Mississippi in 1864—that time he bested the legendary Confederate cavalryman Nathan Bedford Forrest.

But the sixteen-day raid through Mississippi must have been

Colonel Grierson on a rearing steed graced the cover of the country's most widely read publication one month after the most strategically important cavalry operation of the entire Civil War. HARPER'S WEEKLY

indelibly etched in the troopers' minds. July 1863—the surrender of Vicksburg and Lee's defeat at Gettysburg—was the turning point of the war. There was no real doubt after that; those victories assured eventual Federal victory over the rebellion. And there is no doubt that Grierson's brigade was pivotal in turning the tide. Years after, Benjamin Grierson reflected on the raid's importance and why it succeeded: "A wail of humiliation was muttering at home, while abroad many nations smiled on the rebel pirate flag and pointed the finger of derision at the stars and stripes . . . Suddenly a thrilling chord was struck in a major key by 'Grierson's raid.' "

"THE YANKEES AT BROOKHAVEN"

Front-page editorial from *The Daily Mississippian*, April 30, 1863

We have information that the enemy entered Brookhaven yesterday evening, burnt the railroad depot, cut the wires, and after doing what other damage they pleased, leisurely retired (a portion of them at least) in an *easterly* direction . . . Well, well! we are free to admit that Mr. (we beg his pardon) Colonel Grierson and his boys have had a "good time of it" for the past week. It is actually amusing to think (although we confess, annoying) how they have roved around, within forty or fifty miles of the Capitol of the State—eating fried ham and eggs and broiled spring chickens every morning for breakfast, at the expense of the planters whom they choose to honor with a visit—luxuriating on fat mutton, green peas and (of course) strawberries and cream for dinner—and all this without caring for the terrible fact (confound their impudence) that they were within a few hours ride of Lieutenant General John C. Pemberton's headquarters, or thinking for an instant that the commander-in-chief of the "State Troops" lived, moved, breathed and had his being in the city of Jackson. It is actually provoking to think how Colonel (we mean Brigadier General—begging his pardon) Grierson and his jolly riders have enjoyed themselves for a whole week. Why it is really worth a ten months' furlough of a Confederate soldier, this pleasure excursion of the roving blades of Iowa and Illinois in the heart of the "Sunny South!" The fun they must have enjoyed is actually enviable!

We hope Maj. Gen. Grierson (we have a penchant for military titles) will not take off the wires of the telegraph as he proceeds—for, as it seems he can't be caught or headed off, we feel some curiosity to be regularly informed of his whereabouts.

CHAINS OF COMMAND, 1863

NORTH

Abraham Lincoln, president of the United States and commander in chief of the U.S. Army, Washington, D.C.

General Henry W. Halleck, commanding general of the U.S. Army, Washington, D.C.

Major General Ulysses S. Grant, commander of the Department of Tennessee. Grant directed all military offensives in Tennessee, Arkansas, and Mississippi.

Admiral David Porter, U.S. Navy, commander of the Mississippi River Squadron, attached to Grant's forces.

General Stephen A. Hurlbut, commander of the Sixteenth Army Corps, Memphis, Tennessee.

General Christopher C. Augur, commander of land forces at Baton Rouge, Louisiana.

Colonel Benjamin H. Grierson, commander of the First Cavalry Brigade of the Sixteenth Army Corps, La Grange, Tennessee.

Colonel Edward Hatch, commander of the Second Iowa Cavalry Regiment.

Colonel Reuben Loomis, commander of the Sixth Illinois Cavalry Regiment.

Colonel Edward Prince, commander of the Seventh Illinois Cavalry Regiment.

Lieutenant Colonel William Blackburn, battalion commander in the Seventh Illinois.

Major John Graham, battalion commander in the Seventh Illinois.

Captain Jason Smith, commander of Battery K in the First Illinois Artillery.

Captain Henry C. Forbes, commander of Company B in the Seventh Illinois.

Captain George Trafton, commander of Company G in the Seventh Illinois.

Lieutenant James Gaston, Seventh Illinois.

Lieutenant William H. Styles, Seventh Illinois.

Sergeant Stephen A. Forbes, Company B, Seventh Illinois.

Sergeant Richard Surby, quartermaster of the Seventh Illinois, also a Butternut Guerrilla.

Sergeant Lyman Pierce, Second Iowa.

Corporal Samuel Nelson, Seventh Illinois, also a Butternut Guerrilla.

SOUTH

Jefferson Davis, president of the Confederate States of America, Richmond, Virginia.

General Joseph E. Johnston, commander of the Western Department, Chattanooga, Tennessee.

General John C. Pemberton, commander of the Department of Mississippi, Jackson, Mississippi.

General Franklin Gardner, commander at Port Hudson, Louisiana.

General John Bowen, commander at Grand Gulf, Mississippi.

General William Loring, temporary commander of all Confederate troops in northern Mississippi.

General Daniel Ruggles, commander of eastern Mississippi defenses at Columbus, Mississippi.

General James Chalmers, commander of western Mississippi defenses at Panola, Mississippi.

Colonel William Wirt Adams, commander of the First Mississippi Cavalry at Port Hudson.

Colonel Robert V. Richardson, commander of the Twentieth Mississippi Mounted Infantry.

Colonel William R. Miles, commander of Miles's Louisiana Legion.

Lieutenant Colonel Clark Barteau, commander of the Second Tennessee Cavalry.

Major James De Baun, commander of the Ninth Louisiana Partisan Rangers.

Captain Robert C. Love, cavalry commander at Brandon, Mississippi.

Captain Stephen B. Cleveland, cavalry officer at Natchez, Mississippi.

ORGANIZATION OF UNION CAVALRY

Company or troop: The smallest cavalry unit. Fully staffed, a troop would have 105 soldiers. Led by a captain, it would include two lieutenants; eight sergeants; eight corporals; two teamsters, or wagon-team drivers; two farriers, or blacksmiths; two musicians; one saddle repairer; one wagon repairer; and seventy-eight privates.

Squadron: Two troops.

Battalion: Two squadrons.

Regiment: Three battalions. A regiment was led by a colonel. His staff included a lieutenant colonel; three majors; a surgeon; an adjutant, or communications officer; a quartermaster officer, who looked after the rations, ammunition, and other regimental supplies; a commissary officer responsible for food; a chaplain; two hospital stewards; and up to four sergeants with various regimental responsibilities.

Brigade: Three to six regiments, depending on actual troop strength of each regiment.

Division: Three or more cavalry brigades would be grouped with infantry brigades in a division.

ORGANIZATION OF CONFEDERATE CAVALRY

The Confederate States of America followed roughly the same organizational structure as the Union cavalry but not as strictly. By 1863, individual states had organized their own home defense forces. Rangers operated on horseback throughout the South. Not part of the regular army, these partisans raided behind enemy lines and harassed Union troop movement. Northerners commonly called these cavalrymen "guerrillas" or, worse, "bushwhackers."

During the 1863 Mississippi campaign, Grierson encountered all these mixed forces, fighting separately and together. Additionally, his troops were pursued by an organizational unit unique to the Confederate army, a legion. One historian described a legion as "something between a regiment and a brigade." The important organizational factor was personal loyalty to the organizer of the legion unit. William R. Miles's Louisiana Legion attracted a combined force of two thousand infantrymen, three hundred cavalrymen, and a battery of artillery.

CIVIL WAR GLOSSARY

Adjutant: An officer in the army who assists the superior officers by receiving and communicating orders, conducting correspondence, and the like.

Ambuscade: A force placed in ambush. As an intransitive verb: to lie in ambuscade; to ambush.

Barrage: A barrier of continuous artillery or machine-gun fire concentrated in a given area, used to prevent the advance or retreat of enemy troops or to protect troops advancing against the enemy.

Beleaguer: To surround with an army so as to prevent escape.

Bivouac: A temporary encampment of troops in the field with only the accidental shelter of the place, without tents, and so forth; also the place of such encampment.

Blockade: The blockading of essential waterways, inlets, by ships of war. The Federal blockade deprived the Confederacy of much-needed war matériel and prevented the South from selling and moving its cotton abroad.

"Boots and Saddles": A bugle call ordering troopers to their mounts and signaling the alert for cavalrymen to put on their riding boots and saddle their horses for immediate departure.

Border States: Maryland, Kentucky, Delaware, and Missouri. These states were bitterly divided between loyalty to North and South.

Bushwhacker: An irregular or guerrilla soldier who attacks from ambush or in hit-and-run attacks.

Butternut: Many soldiers of the Confederacy wore uniforms colored a yellowish brown by dye made of copperas, iron sulfate in solution, and walnut hulls.

Conscript: A recruit compulsorily enlisted for military or naval service. The Confederacy began conscripting, or drafting, recruits in 1862. The Federal government enacted a draft in 1863.

Demonstration: A show of military force or of offensive movement to engage the enemy's attention while other operations are going on elsewhere or, in time of peace, to indicate readiness for active hostilities.

Feint: A limited attack or movement of troops against one objective to mislead the enemy and cause him to weaken his defenses at the intended point of real attack; more aggressive than a *demonstration*.

Flank: The end or side of a column or line of troops. To flank an enemy position is to get around to its side or rear in order to fire into it.

Forage: Dry winter food for horses, as opposed to grass. Foraging is a roving search for provisions of any kind; sometimes, a raid for ravaging the ground from which the enemy draws his supplies.

Haversack: A white canvas bag about a foot square, carried over the shoulder. It held an enlisted man's food rations and personal property. It had a waterproof lining and a flap that buckled shut.

Home Guards: Locally recruited volunteer forces. Home guards were organized in the South as state units.

Horse-Holder: A trooper assigned the task of controlling a number of mounts when the troops dismount and fight on the ground. Each horse-holder would control four mounts during a skirmish.

Mounted Infantry: Units that ride horses to their destination but fight as infantry.

Parole: An oath a captured soldier made to the enemy in exchange for freedom. The parolee was honor-bound not to fight again until exchanged for an enemy prisoner.

Picket: A small detached body of troops sent out to watch for the approach of the enemy or his scouts; sentinel, outpost.

Point: The small leading party of an advance guard (consisting usually of an experienced noncommissioned officer and several enlisted men).

Quartermaster: An officer or noncommissioned officer attached to each regiment with the duties of providing quarters for the soldiers, laying out the camp, and looking after the rations, ammunition, and other supplies of the regiment.

Reconnoiter: To inspect, examine, or survey (a district or tract of ground) in order to discover the presence or position of an enemy, or to find out the resources or military features of the country.

Skirmish: To engage in a skirmish or irregular encounter; to fight in small parties. A skirmish was smaller than a battle or engagement and larger than an action.

Trestle: A framework consisting of upright (or more or less inclined) pieces with diagonal braces, used to support a bridge or other elevated structure.

BIBLIOGRAPHY

Brown, Dee Alexander. *Grierson's Raid*. Urbana: University of Illinois Press, 1954.

Catton, Bruce. *Never Call Retreat*. Garden City, N.Y.: Doubleday, 1965.

Dinges, Bruce J. "The Making of a Cavalryman: Benjamin H. Grierson and the Civil War along the Mississippi, 1861–1865." Ph.D. diss., Rice University, 1978.

Donald, David, ed. *Why the North Won the Civil War*. Baton Rouge: Louisiana State University Press, 1960.

Forbes, Stephen A. "Grierson's Cavalry Raid." *Transactions of the Illinois State Historical Society* (1907), pp. 99–130.

Grant, Ulysses S. *Personal Memoirs of U. S. Grant*. New York: Library of America, 1990.

Grierson, Benjamin H. "The Lights and Shadows of Life, Including Experiences and Remembrances of the War of the Rebellion." Typescript autobiography. Illinois State Historical Library, Springfield, 1892.

———. *Record of Services Rendered the Government, 1863*. Fort Concho, Tex.: privately printed.

Hattaway, Herman, and Archer Jones. *How the North Won: A Military History of the Civil War*. Urbana: University of Illinois Press, 1983.

Leckie, Shirley A., and William H. Leckie. *Unlikely Warriors: General Benjamin H. Grierson and His Family*. Norman: University of Oklahoma Press, 1984.

McPherson, James M. *For Cause and Comrades: Why Men Fought in the Civil War*. New York: Oxford University Press, 1997.

———. *Ordeal by Fire: The Civil War and Reconstruction*. New York: Alfred A. Knopf, 1982.

Mitchell, Reid. *Civil War Soldiers: Their Expectations and Their Experiences*. New York: Viking, 1988.

Nevins, Allan. *The War for the Union: The Organized War*. New York: Charles Scribner's Sons, 1971.

———. *The War for the Union: War Becomes Revolution, 1862–1863*. New York: Charles Scribner's Sons, 1960.

Surby, Richard W. *Grierson Raids, and Hatch's Sixty-four Days March, with Biographical Sketches, Also the Life and Adventures of Chickasaw, the Scout*. Chicago: Rounds and James, 1865.

Walker, Peter F. *Vicksburg: A People at War, 1860–1865*. Chapel Hill: University of North Carolina Press, 1960.

War of the Rebellion: A Compilation of the Official Records of the Union and Confederate Armies. 128 vols. Washington, D.C.: Government Printing Office, 1880–1901. Available at Cornell University's *Making of America* journal collection: http://cdl.library.cornell.edu/moa/.

Wheeler, Richard. *The Siege of Vicksburg*. New York: Crowell, 1978.

Wiley, Bell Irvin. *The Life of Billy Yank: The Common Soldier of the Union*. Baton Rouge: Louisiana State University Press, 1972.

ACKNOWLEDGMENTS

A number of people have helped make this book possible.

Mary L. Williams, historian of the Fort David National Historical Site, was a font of information about Benjamin H. Grierson and his family.

Les Jensen, curator of small arms and armor at the West Point Museum, provided an invaluable short course in Civil War weaponry. After showing me which weapons the troopers carried, he demonstrated how the weapons worked and explained how highly, or lowly, they were valued by the troopers who carried them.

I thank John Hoffmann of the Illinois Historical Survey of the University of Illinois at Urbana-Champaign; Robert T. Chapel of the University Archives, University of Illinois at Urbana-Champaign; and Jay Graybeal, photo archivist of the U.S. Army Military History Institute for their assistance in unearthing images that enliven the text.

No work of history is possible without the guidance of librarians. My thanks to the staff at the New York Public Library, the Illinois State Historical Library, the University of Southern Mississippi Libraries, and Michele Capozzella, young adult librarian at the Chappaqua, New York, public library, for their resourcefulness in locating and accessing rare books, newspapers, and manuscripts.

I am deeply indebted to Wesley Adams, my editor at Farrar, Straus and Giroux, for enthusiastically embracing the outline of a long-forgotten Civil War story and providing both editorial and historical savvy that added immeasurably to the manuscript.

The stunning design of Nancy Goldenberg and meticulous cartography of David Cain are apparent throughout this work. The copyediting and proofreading contributions of Karla Reganold, Ingrid Sterner, and Karen Ninnis are intentionally invisible, but highly appreciated. Thanks also to Ruth Elwell for creating the index.

Everlasting gratitude is due Barbara Lalicki, always an insightful reader, intelligent critic, and imaginative catalyst.

Allan Nevins, then president of the American Historical Association, wrote that "the scrupulously careful Douglas Freeman once told me with pardonable pride that he had found only about fifty slips in his four-volume *Lee*." I hope that this volume has far fewer errors than that, if only because it is so much shorter than Freeman's works. But whatever errors exist, the reader may be assured that none are the responsibility of any of the previously mentioned persons and institutions.

INDEX